MW00930662

The Jungle

Justin Johnson

The Jungle

Justin Johnson

Copyright © 2016 by CCS Publishing All Rights Reserved.

Cover Copyright © 2016 by CCS Publishing

This is a work of fiction. Any resemblance to actual persons or Fleshbots living or dead, businesses, events, or locales is purely coincidental.

Reproduction, in whole or part, of this publication, without express written consent, is strictly prohibited.

I greatly appreciate you taking the time to read my work. Please consider leaving a review wherever you bought the book, or telling your friends or blog readers about this book, to help me spread the word.

Thank you for supporting my work.

Justin Johnson

GET YOUR FREE BOOK!

For your free copy of the #1 Best Seller Farty Marty, go to www.justinjohnsonauthor.com

BOOK ONE

1

The plane began to shake. The pilot's voice had come over the speaker system an hour earlier and announced something called *turbulence*.

Jake Lennon hadn't been familiar with the term before that moment. But after fifteen minutes of jostling around in his seat, he knew what it was. And he didn't like it.

He didn't like it almost as much as he didn't like the idea of being on this plane in the first place. The seats were cramped, even for a boy of ten.

The plane was a mere commuter jet, at least that's what he'd heard his mother say. There were maybe fifty seats, and half of them weren't even full.

The food was horrible, and he feared that if they hit another bout of 'the turbulence', that he would have to taste it again. Only this time, it would be on the way up and out.

"Please turn off all cell phones and other communication devices," the pilot's voice commanded.

Jake had his headphones on at the time. He didn't hear the announcement, but his father thought that he was just being difficult and took his phone away. His father stuffed it into his pocket and handed Jake an issue of a magazine he'd gotten from the back of the seat in front of him, which Jake could tell would be useless and boring.

He could hardly blame his father for thinking that he was being difficult. He'd been difficult all morning. When they'd told him about the family vacation to South America three weeks earlier, he'd been less than enthusiastic.

The thought of family vacations, or anything that took him out of his bedroom for more than an hour, made Jake a little grumpy. There was nothing he'd rather do than play video games with his friends. And video games weren't going to be available to him on this trip. According to his parents, this was going to be a real 'wilderness' experience.

"That sounds like it's going to be a lot of fun," Jake had said. These had been the words his parents had been hoping to hear, but the tone was not. Rather than excitement, Jake had decided to fill this sentence with snark and sarcasm. His parents had secretly debated whether they should let Jake just stay with his Uncle Tommy for the week. But eventually, they decided that it would be good for him to get out and experience something real. Plus it would be a good bonding experience for the family.

So far, thanks to Jake's father taking his phone away, and all of the turbulence, the vacation was off to a very bumpy start.

And now that the plane was shaking again, Jake was just trying to do whatever he could to ensure that he made it to the ground without anything else going wrong.

"Are you okay?" his father asked. "You don't look so good. Do you feel like you're going to be sick?"

He glared at his father. "Of course I feel sick, the plane's moving up and down like a roller coaster."

"Here," his mother said. She was reaching out her hand, which was holding a small plastic cup full of an amber colored liquid. "It's Ginger Ale. It'll help."

Jake shook his head 'no' and pushed the cup back toward his mother. A large jolt sent the cup flying from his mother's hands and onto his father's lap. Much to Jake's surprise, his father didn't say a word. Rather, he gritted his teeth and blew a tremendous amount of air through his nose.

It sounded like he might have been getting ready to give Jake a stern talking to, when there was a crash. It was loud and sudden. The plane jerked to the right, forcing Jake to look out the window.

He had to rub his eyes and do a double take before he could be sure about the source of the noise. But after a few moments he realized that the wing on his side of the plane had fallen off.

2

Jake stared in disbelief at what was left of the plane's right wing. It was a mess of mangled and curled up metal and wires.

He brought his attention back inside the plane. His father was still looking upset about the ginger ale spill and his mother was apologizing, saying it was all her fault.

The other passengers looked to be coping with the turbulence. They had their hands on their arm rests, and while some of them had white knuckles from holding on tightly, most of them seemed fine.

How could they just sit here and act like nothing had happened?

Had they not heard the crash?

Had they not looked out the window to see for themselves that the wing had broken free and fallen off?

There was another crash and Jake could see sparks and flames outside the left side of the plane. He had a sinking feeling inside that the other wing had just been ripped off by something outside — a lightning bolt, perhaps.

He reached down and unfastened his seat belt.

"Buckle yourself back up," his father said, eyeing him.

"But there's..." Jake stood up to survey the rest of the plane, letting his words trail off.

Nobody. Not a single person was doing anything that would indicate that the plane was on the verge of going down.

"Honey," his mother chimed in, "why don't you do what your father says and sit down?"

Jake turned toward the back of the plane. He could feel his father's hand on his arm, pulling him back down into his seat.

And then he saw her. She was sitting near the back of the plane on the left. Her blond haired pig tails and pink Dora bag gave Jake the impression that she couldn't have been any older than four or five.

She was in a panic. A woman next to her was trying to calm her down, shoving books and small packages of fruit snacks in front of her face.

Jake's father pulled him back into his seat before he could see whether the woman's attempts to distract the girl were successful.

"What's going on with you?" Jake's father asked.

"There's something happening —"

His answer was cut short by another cry of sorts. This time, it was more of a scream, coming from the front of the plane, a few seats ahead of Jake.

"What's gotten into him?" A man asked. His voice had an edge to it, but he seemed more concerned than angry.

"I don't know," A woman answered. "He was fine just a moment ago."

The boy continued to scream, gaining the attention of the flight attendant. A portly man in a blue vest shuffled up the aisle toward the family, his hips rubbing the edges of the seats as he made his way. He had a stern look on his face, which was becoming redder with every step he took. By the time he reached the family, he was breathing heavily and had to take a moment to compose himself before speaking.

"Son," he said, addressing the boy and not his parents. "Excuse me." He waited and watched as the boy continued his fit. "Young man!" the attendant finally boomed.

The boy continued to scream and shout. And now his father joined him, standing up and directing every ounce of his ire toward the attendant, whose eyes had the appearance of tea saucers.

"You will not speak to my son like that! If you have any problem with anyone in my family, you speak with me!"

The attendant's mouth dropped open and hung numbly from the his face. He shook his head back and forth, looking for help, as his jowls swayed from side to side. Another flight attendant came walking toward the situation from the front of the plane.

"What seems to be the problem?" She asked. She was thin with brown hair that hung in a tight braid down the middle of her back. She wore the same airline issued uniform as the man, but hers fit better.

The first attendant tried to update her on the situation, but his mouth still wasn't working. "Ub...a...eh...this...er..."

She put a finger up in the air and turned to the angry passenger.

"Sir, could you please help me understand what's going on here?"

Before he could get out a response, Jake felt the plane begin its descent.

3

The descent was swift. Not at all like landing, but more like the plane was going to crash. Heading toward the ground that fast could yield only one result.

Jake continued to look around, wondering why only he and the two kids, whose cries of fear were deafening, were noticing that the plane was going down.

Jake turned to the back of the plane and spotted the little girl with the Dora backpack.

She'd curled up like a ball, her head tucked deep in her bag, her feet and legs closing her off from the rest of the world.

And then there was the situation with the flight attendants up front.

Oddly, as everybody craned their necks to get a good view of the show, nobody seemed to notice that the plane was headed toward earth at a rapid rate. They continued to eat their airline chicken and drink their warm soda, but were generally unconcerned.

Jake looked at his own parents, who were looking at him.

"Are you doing better now?" his father asked. He had a grin on his face and nodded in the direction of the boy in front of them. "You know, Jake, sometimes I don't give you enough credit. I see boys like that, who have no idea how to behave in public, and I can't help but think... you're a pretty great kid." He sat back in his seat, puffing his chest out with pride, a satisfied look on his face.

"Dad," Jake said, "don't you know why they're acting like that?"

"Nope. And I don't care." He gave Jake a wink.

"The plane's going down, dad." Jake turned to his mother. "Don't you feel that mom?"

"Now that's ridiculous!" His father said quietly, so as not to draw any attention.

Jake looked out the window again and there was a flash of light. It was a wide band of white light that seemed to envelope every side of the plane, like it was flying through a ring of fire.

It lasted little more than a second, and again, Jake could tell the boy and little girl had seen it, and the adults had not.

When the light had subsided, and Jake was no longer seeing floating spots, he looked out the window. Horror filled his heart as his lungs evacuated themselves of any air.

The last thing Jake Lennon saw was the tops of the trees, just before the plane hit them, and his mother looking at him through concerned eyes. He was conscious when she asked, "Jake? Are you alright?"

And then he wasn't.

4

Jake came to slowly. His eyelids were heavy. When he finally managed to get them open, there was a sheen over his eyes, like vaseline smeared on a lens. The first thing he noticed was how dark it was. He instinctively put his hand out, reaching and feeling around for anything he might recognize as familiar.

He was on his back and the first thing he felt was the smooth armrest of the seat that had been across the aisle from his own.

Pulling himself up, he stood on the side wall of the plane, straddling a tiny window.

Jake thought for a minute, trying to get his bearings. For him to be standing here, in this spot, and not falling over, the plane would have to be tipped on its side.

He looked down through the window and could see dirt and leaves — the ground. When he looked up, he saw a mix of dense vegetation blocking out the blue, sun streaked sky.

He shook his head.

That couldn't be. Could it?

It took Jake a moment to look down again, but when he did, it confirmed his initial fears that the plane was not on the ground. Rather, it was suspended in the air. And from the looks of it, Jake estimated that it was, at least, a fifteen foot drop, maybe more.

Where was his mother?

Where was his father?

As he was wondering where everyone else might be, he heard a groan. It was soft and high, like that of a small child.   And then Jake remembered the girl.

Was she still here?

He held onto what had been his father's armrest and pulled himself up to look toward the back of the plane. He moved slowly at first, feeling the plane rocking back and forth with each and every movement he made, no matter how subtle. He half walked, half crawled over a half a dozen seats to make his way back to where the girl was sitting, no doubt scared out of her mind.

"Are you alright?" he whispered to the girl, though he didn't know why he was whispering. They were, seemingly, in the middle of nowhere.

"Where's mommy?" the girl whimpered.

Jake could hear the tears in her voice.

The girl was sitting with her knees up to her chin, square in the middle of the window.

Jake's mind was racing, trying to put all these pieces of information together into one coherent and logical thought.

Jake took a second and stole a glance toward the front of the plane, wishing he'd done this earlier, though he wasn't sure it would've changed anything.

There was a rather large tree branch coming through the cabin door, where the pilots would've been sitting while flying the plane. The door remained closed, but the branch had broken through and made its way about half the length of the aisle.

The plane is in a tree, Jake found himself thinking.

His breathing picked up.

He was hyperventilating.

And then he heard the sound that had gotten him back here in the first place.

The girl.

Crying.

Instantly, Jake had forgotten about the fear that gripped him deep within and he focused his energy on her.

"It's okay," Jake said, attempting to comfort the girl. "Don't move. I'll come down to get you."

"Don't," the girl said.

"Why not?"

"Because…"

"Because why?" Jake asked with more agitation in his voice that he'd meant.

"Because, I'll fall."

The girl leaned her body to one side, slowly. There was a crack above the window. It was jagged and as Jake followed it with his eyes, he could see that it went all the way around the plane, almost as though they'd gone through a giant can opener on the way down.

Jake knew it was just a matter of time before the back of the plane let loose and the girl plummeted to ground below. He had to think of something…and fast.

5

Jake's head was pounding.

Where were they?

How did they get here?

Where was everybody?

Who was this girl?

And, how in the heck was he going to get her out of this predicament?

He looked around for something to extend to her. In the seat closest to him there was a seat belt, still buckled, as if the passenger who'd previously had that seat was still sitting in it.

Reaching over slowly, Jake unbuckled the belt and took the adjustable end in his hands. He worked the metal clasp to the end of the belt, making it as long as it could possibly be; three or four feet, he'd guessed.

"Listen to me," he said to the girl.

She looked up.

It was the first time Jake had really stopped to notice her eyes. They were pale blue like that of a doll's. They were bloodshot from crying.

"I'm going to throw this belt down to you. Grab on and I'll pull you up."

The girl nodded slowly.

Jake dropped the long end of the seat belt. The metal end sailed past the girl and hit the glass of the window, which began spidering, slowly at first, and then rapidly.

The girl looked down and watched in horror as the lines made their way toward the outer edge of the window.

Without further warning the glass gave way, completing the break in the plane. The back of the plane fell suddenly to the ground and Jake saw the girl free fall.

He reached his hand out for her, though he knew he was too far away to do anything.

The girl instinctively reached her hand up and grabbed hold of the seat belt.

Her grip was strong enough to hold onto the belt, but not strong enough to keep her from sliding down and out the void left by the break.

"Hold tight!" Jake yelled. "I'm going to pull you up."

A shadow moved below the girl.

Something Jake couldn't make out.

He just hoped that he could get her back up into the plane before he had to deal with whatever was out there.

And then he saw another shadow.

And another.

And then a streak of orange.

And then the pale blue eyes of the girl, just before they shot up at him and she began to scream.

6

Jake was trying frantically to get his hands around the seat belt.

It was synched so tightly against the back of the seat it was attached to, that he didn't think he could get it without tipping the whole plane.

"We're stable here."

Jake took his eyes off the girl and looked toward the front of the plane, where a boy in a gray hoodie was pulling himself up against one of the seats, and trying to make his way toward Jake and the girl.

Jake guessed that the boy was telling him it was alright to move to save the girl.

This advice didn't come a moment too soon.

When Jake looked down, he could see the biggest of the tigers leaping up and narrowly missing the girl's shoes. There were three of them in all. They were big and they were mean, licking their lips and sniffing the air.

"I'm going to jump down," he said to the girl. "You need to hang on really tight."

The girl gave an affirmative nod and gripped onto the belt even tighter, like she was wringing the life out of it.

Jake jumped, landing with both feet on the jagged edge left by the back of the plane's absence.

From this position, Jake could easily grab the seat belt.

Pulling the girl up, on the other hand, proved to be a challenge.

The tigers continued their circular path below, their tongues licking around their snout, waiting for the moment when the girl's body met the dirt and they got to eat.

"Don't look down at them," Jake said to the girl. "Just concentrate on holding on tight."

Jake pulled the girl up slowly, praying under his breath that he could hold the weight of her long enough to get her to safety.

The boy from the front was making his way toward them both, climbing over the seats quickly, the plane shaking back and forth with his every step.

Jake forced himself to ignore this and got the girl to the sharp edges of the plane. He kept the seat belt in one hand and reached toward the girl with the other. She looked tentative at first, but reached for his free hand anyway. Jake pulled her up slowly, making sure that she didn't get cut by the shards of metal that were dangling from the severed section. The girl was able to get her shoes up and onto one of the seats before being pulled all the way to safety.

She shuffled over toward Jake, out of clear view of the tigers below. She was whimpering.

"It's okay. We're okay. We're all okay," Jake said, trying to calm her.

The boy had made his way back, now laying, belly down, across the seats and staring down at Jake and the girl.

"What's your name?" he asked.

"I'm Jake."

The girl looked up but didn't speak.

They were safe and as Jake looked back out the window, he could see the tigers retreating back into the dense forest.

"That was nuts! What's your name?" Jake asked the boy.

"Terrance."

Terrance looked to be a little older than Jake, maybe eleven or twelve. He had dark eyes, that were made darker by the presence of his hood. He put his hand out to shake Jake's. Jake noticed that Terrance had a very strong grip.

"Nice to meet you Terrance. Say, do you have any idea what's going on here?"

"Not a clue. All I know is we landed hard and now we're here."

"Well, the three of us will have to help take care of each other, from the looks of things."

Terrance nodded.

And then from somewhere near the front of the plane, they heard a groan.

7

Jake didn't waste anytime getting back on top of the seats and climbing in the direction of the groans. He moved quickly, nudging Terrance out of the way.

When he finally got to the source of the noise, he saw a boy who was still buckled into his seat, his head and arms hanging over an armrest.

The boy was small and mousey.

Jake remembered him from earlier. He had raised such a ruckus that the flight attendants had been called over, which resulted in a rather uncomfortable scene for everyone on board.

"Hey," Jake said, "give me your hand and I'll help you down."

"Where's my mommy?" the boy asked.

"We don't really know," Terrance answered, now crawling up next to Jake. "Everyone disappeared when the plane went down and we're the only ones left....well, us and all those animals."

Jake rolled his eyes a little.

"What?" Terrance asked, sensing a tinge of frustration in Jake's face.

"Wait for it..."

The boy in the seat began to wail and sob.

"Sorry," Terrance said, now realizing the error of his ways. "I guess we should have waited until we got him down from there before we mentioned the whole missing parent thing."

"Yeah, I guess," said Jake.

The boy in the seat curled up into a little ball now, hiding his face from the other two boys.

Jake gave Terrance a little nod and glance toward the rear of the plane.

He understood and the two began moving back toward the girl.

As they'd predicted, the boy in the seat began to come around.

"Wait...don't go! I'll be good! I'll come down!"

Jake couldn't help but smile a little as he turned back around to offer the boy a hand.

The boy unbuckled his seat belt, grabbed Jake's hand and fell, somewhat gracefully, to the opposite aisle seat.

"So, what do we do now?" the boy asked.

Terrance and Jake looked at each other.

"We get out of here," Jake answered.

8

The front of the plane.

That would be the best way.

The back of the plane was already open, but it was about a fifteen foot drop to the ground. If they could somehow get close enough to the tree that had come through the front, they would be able to climb their way down to the ground.

Jake and Terrance helped the girl and the boy up onto the branch and guided them to the front of the plane.

"I don't know how we're going to get through this door," said Jake, pointing to the cockpit. He was inspecting it, noting that there would be no way they would be able to shift the door on its hinges due to the position of the tree branch. Craning his neck over the edge of the branch, Jake saw the door and staircase everyone had used to board the plane. Because the plane had been tipped, it was now pointing in the direction of the ground.

This could be promising.

"Wait here," he ordered.

Jake dropped himself gingerly onto the flight attendant's seat, which was tucked just inside main doorway of the plane.

He wrapped the seat belt around his wrist, making sure he had a tight grip on it before he let himself down to the door.

There was no window in the door.

"I'm going to kick it open," he called up to the others. "Be ready to head in the other direction if anything unexpected comes through."

Terrance nodded. The girl's eyes started to water again. And the other boy didn't react one way or the other.

Palms sweaty, Jake placed both hands on the handle and began to turn it toward the floor of the plane. It turned harder than he'd expected. In a way it made him feel an odd sense of security that the door on a plane wouldn't just fly open during the plane's flight. And then he stopped himself, realizing how stupid this thought was, after the plane had already crash landed in a tree in the middle of the jungle, leaving him stranded with only three other kids.

When the handle was perfectly perpendicular to the floor, Jake heard a *click*. He still had the seat belt wrapped around his arm, and he had his toes propped along the outer edge of the door, not wanting to put too much pressure on it too soon.

He looked up at Terrance. "Are you ready?"

Terrance nodded.

Jake put his full weight on the door and felt it descend open slowly. The hydraulics were still in tact, which allowed Jake to gradually release his arm from the seat belt.

His eyes were wide as he lowered down into the unknown wilderness.

He knew they were high enough up to avoid the tigers or any of the other animals that might be rendered ground bound. But he had to keep his senses sharp until he could definitively tell that there were no tree dwelling threats.

The thick green leaves snapped up as the door continued to lower, the branches hitting Jake in the face on their way back to their original positions.

Jake was relieved to think that there would be something to hold onto when they climbed out of the plane. But these leaves were so thick and dense that Jake's view of the actual tree, and anything that might be hidden in it, was greatly diminished.

When the door finally stopped moving, Jake allowed his grip on the seat belt to relax. He crouched himself down onto the small set of stairs that were built into the door and looked hard out into the wilderness.

"Don't move," he warned the others.

Jake felt a chill go through his body. Something inside was telling him that there was danger. He could feel it, just under his skin, sending all the hairs on his body straight up to attention.

And that's when he saw them.

Just beyond the first wave of leaves, tucked away and concealed.

A set of eyes.

Yellow.

And staring right at him.

9

"Do you see anything?" Terrance asked.

He'd noticed that Jake had stopped and all the color had flushed from his face, leaving him a pale stone statue on the bottom step of the door.

When Jake didn't answer, Terrance started moving the boy and the girl toward the back of the plane.

"What is it?" the girl asked.

"I'm not sure, but I think Jake can handle it," Terrance said, trying to reassure the girl that no more harm would come their way, though he couldn't be sure.

The girl moved quickly. The boy was a different story.

"Come on," Terrance said. "It's okay, buddy. We're going to be okay. We just have to move toward the back, that's all."

The boy finally moved, though it was slow and deliberate.

Terrance let out a small sigh, half relief and half frustration.

"Stop," he said when the girl had almost reached the end of the branch. "Just sit tight for a moment." The boy was just between them and Terrance was still located close to the doorway, waiting in position for Jake to give him a sign one way or another.

"How is it out there, Jake?" he asked.

No response.

He took a quick scoot toward the door and leaned back to get a view of where Jake had been.

The seat belt was still taught, like someone was pulling on it from the other side of the door.

The door was closed.

And Jake was still outside.

10

The snake moved slowly through the branches.

Jake panicked and slipped. He was hanging by the seat belt wrapped around his wrist. The hydraulics, which had allowed him to slowly emerged from the plane, now worked against him and snapped the door shut.

He kicked his feet, trying to find the edge of the plane. It was hard to get his footing on the surface because of its round exterior.

Finally, his right foot caught and he was able to brace himself against the outer wall of the plane, like a mountain climber on a harness.

He lost sight of the snake's bright yellow eyes for a moment.

Searching frantically, sweating, he was breathing heavy, though he was trying to keep quiet. He had to find those eyes; had to know where they were.

The leaves seemed thicker, more opaque than before.

Breathe slower, he told himself. *Calm down.*

Finding those eyes in the midst of the foliage seemed impossible.

Jake squinted and rubbed his eyes, trying to keep the sweat from his forehead at bay. If the sweat got into his eyes he might as well be a goner out here.

And then he heard it.

The kick of a rattle and the hiss of the snake.

And it wasn't far away.

He sensed it now, and wished that it hadn't taken until then to locate it.

The top of his head was warm and as he looked up, the snake's tongue was flicking in and out, inches from his face.

Jake instinctively let go of the belt and allowed himself to drop, not caring how far down he'd fall.

But he didn't fall as far as he thought before his arm was given a sudden jerk.

The belt was still wrapped around his wrist and when he kicked off the side of the plane and allowed his body to go limp, he swung back and struck the plane hard with his face.

It took all the strength and concentration he could muster to keep the tears from coming. He twisted his arm, trying to let go of the belt, spinning around in a circle as the strong cloth released its grip.

The snake was now slithering over the edge of the plane, the majority of its long scaly body was moving forward over the branch that had impaled the plane's front windshield.

Jake glanced up for a second and got a good look at the sharp fangs as the snake opened its mouth and lunged forward.

The final piece of the seat belt came loose and Jake went falling to the ground, teeth barely missing his head.

He hit the ground with a thud and felt a searing pain in his arm.

Lying there on the ground, trying to catch his breath, he made out a movement in the distance.

He was feeling dizzy and his eyes were a little glazed over from the fall, but he could definitely see something moving in the bushes up ahead.

Streaks of orange and black blurred together as the beast emerged from the bushes and moved toward him.

11

Terrance scrambled across the branch until he could see out one of the passenger windows. He dropped down and stared in horror as the tiger crept its way over to where Jake was lying motionless.

"Stay still," he whispered.

"Is that tiger going to hurt him," the girl asked from over Terrance's shoulder.

"I don't know."

The plane began to shake and there was a loud series of thumps.

Terrance looked around, wondering what could be making the noise. He turned and saw fear in the two children sitting on the branch.

"It's okay," he said, not entirely sure that it would be.

When he turned back to the window, he saw that it was blocked by a scaly mass.

"This is not good."

"What's not good," the girl asked.

"That noise," Terrance said, pointing up.

"What is it?"

"Just stay where you are and don't move."

Terrance didn't want to scare her unless it was necessary.

12

The warm breath from the beast was upon him.

Jake didn't dare open his eyes, for fear of seeing what might destroy him. It was easier to just keep his eyes closed and hope that the giant tiger decided to give up and walk away.

He'd seen people play dead before and live to tell about it when a bear had been attacking them.

But those were always on TV, in movies or shows.

And always with bears.

And this wasn't TV.

And this wasn't a bear.

The tiger circled, sniffing and breathing as it went. Every so often, Jake would feel a paw pushing his feet back and forth. Jake tried to make his body as limp and lithe as possible, just in case playing dead really worked.

He had somehow managed to slow his breathing down. If he had any chance of fooling this behemoth he would have to be as convincing as possible.

After a few minutes, it seemed as though the tiger had given up on him. The warm heavy breaths had ceased and there was no longer any intermittent touchings from the tiger's paw.

Jake was starting to think he was in the clear.

And then he heard a large thud behind him.

13

Jake could feel the ground vibrate beneath the slithering body of the snake.

It had dropped down from the top of the plane and now it was making it's way over to where Jake was lying motionless.

He could hear the snake's rattle, making its presence known.

It only took a moment before he felt the snake's tongue licking the back of his neck. It was moving back and forth quickly.

Jake's heart was beating hard in his chest and he could feel his breathing hastening again.

"Jake!"

He heard the shout coming from above him, but he didn't dare open his eyes to look, nor his mouth to speak.

"Get ready to run!"

It was Terrance.

Run?

Run where?

How?

There was no way he would be able to make it out of here alive, was there? And even if he did, where would he go?

"I'm going to tell you when to go! You're going to run to your left and into the trees, toward the front of the plane!"

Should he trust Terrance? What were his options? If he didn't trust Terrance and go for it, he'd probably be a goner anyway.

He had no way to tell Terrance that he'd understood what he was saying.

They would have to trust each other.

Jake took a second and tried to figure out how he was going to be able to push himself up off the ground with his arm hurting like it was. If he'd broken it, pushing himself up would only help to further the amount of damage done. He'd have to roll over slightly on top of it and then push himself up with his right arm in order to get to his feet.

"Go!"

Terrance's voice rang through the air and Jake rolled just as he'd planned. The pain shot through his arm and into his body, burning and stinging in a way he couldn't prepare himself for. He winced with pain and then opened his eyes.

He didn't know which hurt worse, his arm or his eyes. They were flooded instantly with bright sunlight, cutting through the branches. Sweat dripped down from his forehead.

His legs were feeling like jello as he tried to run, wobbly and unstable. He felt himself veering to the left and then to right as he struggled to find his footing.

Finally, things snapped into place and he felt himself gathering speed, pumping his right arm up and down, keeping his left arm tight to his side as though it was tethered.

Using his shoulder and shirt, he managed to wipe enough sweat from his eyes to be able to see.

He was running straight for a group of thick trunked trees.

A place to hide.

When he'd arrived at the first tree, he ducked behind it and turned around. Cautiously, he maneuvered his body and head to the side and took a peek toward the opening from which he'd come.

He was astonished to see the tiger had friends. All three of them had now come back. They were locked in a battle with the humongous snake, which Jake could now see in all of its glory. It had to be a least a hundred feet long, and six or seven feet wide at the thickest part of its body.

It was lunging at the tigers, keeping them at bay.

After a moment or so, the tigers started to coordinate an attack plan and two of the tigers were sent to the outer edges of where the snake would be able to see.

Jake looked around, thinking that this might not be the best place to be if one of those beasts decided to retreat. They were fighting over him, after all.

There were branches sticking out of the trunk of the tree he now found himself at the base of. He could easily see a way that he could climb up and get himself out of harm's way.

When he'd climbed about fifteen feet or so, he stopped and looked down. He could see Terrance watching the brawl from the broken edge on the plane, where the girl had been trying to avoid the tigers moments earlier. Terrance gave him a thumbs up. Jake returned it and then brought his eyes back to the battle.

The snake had put up a valiant fight, but in the end the tigers overtook him with two sneak attacks from the sides. They had lunged and sank their tremendous teeth into the back of the snake's head. While they were doing this, the front tiger moved forward and chomped down on the snake's mouth, keeping the giant reptile's teeth concealed like a muzzle.

The snake's tail flopped around, creating a tremendous amount of dust, which made it difficult to see anything. The ground shook, as did the trees surrounding the clearing. Jake grabbed on tight.

The white knuckle ride lasted a few moments before the snake succumbed to it's injuries.

Jake felt safe in the tree for the moment, but knew it would only be a matter of time before he encountered something else.

With that thought in his mind, he began the traverse across the trees toward the plane. And this time, there was nothing that was going to stop him from getting everyone out.

14

"Grab my hand!"

Jake was on his stomach at the tail end of the plane, leaning over the frayed edge and extending his arm toward the others.

"You first," Terrance said, grabbing the girl by the waist and trying to hand her up to Jake while keeping his balance on the seats. The girl grabbed onto an armrest and then Jake's hand and was pulled out.

The boy, on the other hand, was less willing to make the climb to the top of the aircraft.

"I don't want to," he whined. "It's safer in here."

"That may be," said Terrance. "But in here, there's no way out of wherever we are. You're not going to get the plane working again. We have no grown ups to help us. We're on our own."

He put his hand out for the boy, who still refused to grab hold.

"Suit yourself," Terrance said, hoisting himself upward toward Jake's hand.

"No! I'm coming, I'm coming!"

The boy moved faster than he had the entire time. He had to stop for a minute and wipe the tears from his eyes with his shirt sleeve. Then Terrance took him and helped him get to a place where Jake could help him up.

Terrance then climbed up himself.

The four of them stood on top of the plane surveying their situation.

They were in the middle of a small clearing, twenty feet off the ground. Thick trees all around and nothing in sight that would give them so much as a hint about how they'd gotten there.

"What's your name?" Jake asked the girl.

"Hainey," she replied.

He knelt down and put his hands on her shoulders. "Hainey, I don't know what happened to your mother, but I'm going to try to help you find her. Okay?"

She nodded.

Next, he went to the boy. "And what's your name?"

"Max."

Jake again knelt down and put his hands on the boy's shoulders. "Max, I don't know what happened to your parents, but I'm going to try to help you find them. Okay?"

Max nodded.

Jake stood up and extended his hand to Terrance.

"Thanks for all your help. I'm not sure I would have gotten through that on my own."

"No problem," Terrance smirked.

Jake looked off into the trees, listening to the sounds of nature. Some of them were soothing, while others were uninviting and frightening.

He looked at Hainey and Max, feeling a deep sense of responsibility to them. He had to find their parents and he had to find his own. Terrance, no doubt would be looking for his.

"I've got a question for you Terrance?"

"What's that?" Terrance replied, looking down at the tigers, who were celebrating their kill below.

"Where do we go from here?"

BOOK TWO

1

Jake Lennon woke with a start.

He moved his head from side to side, trying to make out anything in the distance. But it was too dark to see.

Terrance had promised Jake earlier that this place would be safe.

They had left the safety of the plane and walked for hours in a northern direction. At least that's what Terrance's compass had read.

Terrance had sat down and proclaimed, "This is the best spot we're going to find out here. Let's settle in and get some rest."

Jake had asked Terrance the same question then that he was asking himself now: How could they be so sure that this place would be safe?

It didn't look that different from any of the other places they'd seen since starting their journey. Dense vegetation and thick tree trunks were in abundance. Small bushes and twigs brushed up against their legs and feet, giving Jake an uneasy feeling about things.

They had walked for what must've been two hours after climbing down from the plane and managed to avoid further rendezvous with any other fearsome animals.

And they were tired.

Jake was worried that they had let fatigue goad them into making a poor decision. He thought that, perhaps, when Terrance said this was the perfect place, what he was really saying was that he was too tired to continue.

Hainey and Max had been whiney and neither Terrance nor Jake cared to listen to it anymore.

So they sat down at the base of an old rotted out tree and snuggled tight. Terrance had told them that they could use the heat from their bodies to keep themselves warm without blankets. All they had to do was huddle together.

It was weird at first.

Jake wasn't the touchy feely type, and wrapping his arms around people he'd just met and didn't really know was almost more than he could bear.

It took a while for them to get to sleep. They were dirty and hungry for one. Plus the events of the day were wandering around Jake's mind. At this point, he had more questions than answers.

What had happened to all of their parents?

Would they be able to find them?

Were they alright?

What might happen to them if they never saw their parents again?

Would they ever get out of this jungle?

Eventually, he had managed to calm his mind down enough to get some sleep, though it was light and shallow.

He didn't know how long he'd been sleeping before he'd heard the branch snap in the distance. He was awake again, his defense systems on high alert.

He could feel the sweat forming on the side of his temples and running down his cheeks. The salty taste of it hit his lips.

It was all Jake could do to keep his breathing at bay.

Hainey was fast asleep on his right arm, curled up in a ball, and looking peaceful for the first time since all of this began.

He didn't want to do anything to put her back into a panic if he could help it.

His left hand wandered back and forth, trying to locate Terrance.

Jake could feel a painful and unrelenting throbbing going through his shoulder and upper arm.

Reminders of what had happened earlier with the tigers were something that Jake didn't need. But his arm was going to make sure that he didn't forget.

He felt something in the darkness.

A piece of cloth.

Jake pressed down and felt a leg...or an arm. He couldn't be sure.

It seemed too small to belong to Terrance.

And then he heard Max give a little whimper and the leg or arm beneath the cloth moved, pulling away from Jake's hand.

Where's Terrance?

Could it be that he'd just left them?

Jake felt a wave of heat rush to his face.

That was it, wasn't it? He left them. Got them all settled here in the middle of this place and left.

Jake heard another branch snap.

And then another.

They were breaking faster and faster, the sound getting closer with every snap.

Up ahead, Jake could start to make something out.

It looked like a beam of light.

Was there someone else out here?

He wondered if he should call out, or just sit quietly and wait.

The beam was moving back and forth over the leafy terrain.

Jake sat as quietly as he could. The fear of what was out there was far greater than his desire to find out.

It wasn't an animal. That much was clear.

But what kind of a human it was on the dark end of that flashlight remained to be seen.

Was it possible that they weren't the only humans out here?

The footsteps kept coming.

The closer they got, the faster they came.

The light became brighter, blinding Jake as it moved toward him.

His heart was thumping hard in his chest, and he felt his right arm instinctively tighten around Hainey.

"What are you doing awake?" came a whisper through the light.

Jake recognized the voice instantly.

Terrance.

"That's a good question," Jake replied. "I should be asking you the same."

Terrance knelt down in front of Jake and flashed a light onto his free hand.

Terrance was holding onto a fish. It wasn't large, a foot, maybe less.

"Where'd you find that?"

"There's a stream about fifteen minutes from here on foot. It's loaded with these little guys." Terrance stood up and pointed the flashlight in the direction from which he'd just come. "We should head in that direction as soon as the kids wake up."

"Agreed."

2

"Where are we going again?"

They had been walking less than five minutes and already Max was whining.

"We already told you," Jake said. He had been annoyed when this vacation was presented to him by his parents. And that's when things were going according to plan.

He was going to have a roof over his head, his parents were going to be around and he wouldn't have to struggle to survive with three other kids who had no idea what was going on.

But his annoyance had turned to flat out anger as they walked through the muggy brush, his hunger for both answers and food clawing away at his insides.

Terrance was a little more patient with Max. "There's a stream or river about ten more minutes in this direction. Once we're there we can catch some fish to eat, grab a drink, clean up and try to figure out a game plan for getting out of here."

"Where do you think we are?" Hainey chimed in.

Both kids were starting to become comfortable with Terrance. They were looking at him as a leader; someone they could trust.

Jake, on the other hand, was starting to feel irritated by Terrance. He thought that it might be better if he looked at him as a friend; someone who was able offer him help in his time of need.

But there was something about Terrance that just didn't feel right to Jake.

"Our plane was over South America when we went down," Terrance said. "I don't know how far south or how far inland, but I think it's safe to say that we are in a South American jungle. So plan on being hot and uncomfortable for a little while. And whatever you do, stay close by. We don't know what other kinds of threats exist out here. I have a feeling the tigers and snake were just the beginning of the dangerous creatures tour that we now find ourselves on."

Hainey nodded and grabbed Terrance's hand.

He looked down at her and gave her a quick wink.

Jake was trailing the group. He didn't know where to look or what to look for. But it didn't stop his eyes from darting from high to low; from left to right.

He was scouring the air and ground for any signs of danger. There were none to be seen at the moment, but he wasn't about to take any chances.

As Jake looked around, he thought he had never seen anything so green before. The leaves and bushes in this jungle were most amazing shades of pale and dark greens. And every shade of green in between.

"That's odd," Terrance said, stopping to observe one of the leaves Jake was admiring from a distance.

"What's that?" asked Jake.

"These leaves." Terrance pointed at a large leaf that looked like the floppy ear of a bunny rabbit. It flopped over on itself and had red veiny lines shooting off from the stalk. He hunched over to investigate.

Hainey reached forward trying to get a closer look.

"No," Terrance shouted, holding his hand out toward her. "If this is what I think it is, it's extremely poisonous. You'd be down and dead before you even had a chance to get all of your fingers around it."

The blood rushed from Hainey's face to her feet and she became as white as a piece of paper.

Seeing what his reaction had done to Hainey and Max, Terrance now began to back pedal. "Oh, it's okay. I didn't mean to scare you. It's probably nothing. Let's just make sure nobody touches it though." He stood up and took a deep breath.

"Let's move on," he said, keeping his eyes on the younger kids as they moved past the plant. "Nice and easy now, that's it."

Jake leaned over the plant. He wasn't going to touch it or anything, but he definitely wanted to take a second and see what all the fuss was about.

He had his nose about five inches from the top of the plant and inhaled cautiously.

The plant had a lemony scent to it. Like the kind that his mother's favorite floor cleaner had had.

A feeling in his stomach forced him to step to his right and throw up. Jake didn't know if it was something that had come from the plant or the grief he was feeling from the loss of his parents.

Either way, his already empty stomach became emptier.

He wiped his mouth off with his forearm and caught up to the others.

"Are you okay?" Max asked.

"Yeah," Jake said, trying to stay strong. When he noticed that Terrance was looking at him, he realized how important it was that he didn't look like a wimp. "I'll be okay."

"A few more minutes," Terrance said reassuringly.

Jake nodded and they continued.

3

They arrived at the water without further incident.

Terrance waded in up to his knees, soaking his sneakers and jeans.

Jake looked down at his pants and thought, *no way.*

"Aw, come on!" Terrance chided, noticing how hesitant Jake was to get his clothing wet.

"Uh-uh. No way man. These clothes on my body are the only thing I have out here. There's no way I'm going to just jump into the water and get them all soaking wet!"

"What's the worst that could happen?" Terrance asked. "It's not like we're in a cold place. You're not going to die of hypothermia or anything like that."

"I know —"

"So you might as well jump in and get a little relief from the heat. Plus it would give all of us a little relief from your BO!" Terrance motioned to Hainey and Max, who seemed oblivious to the meaning of the term BO.

Jake smirked and almost cracked a smile for the first time since he'd left his house on this blasted trip.

"Yeah," he said. "Maybe you're right."

He took two steps into the water and was surprised at how warm it was. It was like bath water. It felt good on his legs.

As he waded in a little further, he and Terrance found themselves waist deep in the stream.

Jake looked down and couldn't see the top of the pocket of his pants.

"Terrance?" he asked.

"'Sup buddy," Terrance replied, his hands outstretched and face looking up toward the sun, squinting.

"This water's really dirty. Do you have any idea what else might be in here with us?"

"Sure do," Terrance answered cooly. "Remember that fish I brought back with me this morning?"

"Yeah."

"Well, I know there's at least one of those suckers hanging around in here."

Jake began to feel uneasy.

He looked over toward the shoreline, where Hainey and Max were standing. They were still not quite ready to test the waters.

A fact Jake was happy about.

He looked down again at the murky, brown water surrounding him. How could he have been so stupid?

He was easily fifteen feet away from safety. And if there was anything in here, there was no way either Jake or Terrance would have the faintest idea.

"I'm going to head for land," Jake announced. "Kids," he called to Hainey and Max, who were looking frightened, "stay right there. I'm on my way."

The kids never moved. They continued to look down the stream, away from where Jake and Terrance stood.

The looks on their faces said it all.

There was something down there.

And then Jake looked where they were looking.

Just in time to see a long, scaly tail go under.

4

"Get out of the water! Terrance! Let's go!"

Jake was running toward Hainey and Max. They were his first priority. He had to get to them and help them get to higher ground, or a maybe even a tree.

Terrance stood in the middle of the water, unmoved. His arms still outstretched, eyes toward the sky.

"I mean it Terrance," Jake yelled again, hoping that perhaps his first cries hadn't been heard.

The closer Jake got to the shore, the thicker the silt and mud. He found it difficult to move his feet through and get himself to land despite the urgency he now felt.

He looked back in the tail's direction. The tail wasn't above the water, but there were concentric ripples coming off of both sides of whatever it was that was under there.

They were heading straight for Terrance.

"Last chance man!" Jake yelled. "You have to get out of there!"

It was no use. Terrance wasn't budging.

The kids.

Jake pulled his mud covered feet out of the stream and began to climb up onto the bank.

He looked around for a stick or something long that he could throw out or hold out to Terrance.

Hainey and Max were watching as the shape under the water continued to close the distance between itself and Terrance.

Hainey was crying, as she had on the plane.

Max appeared to be in some kind of shock. He was silent and unmoving.

Jake could find nothing to send in Terrance's direction.

He ran over to where the kids were standing and grabbed them each around the waist.

Neither of the kids resisted his pull on them. But the throbbing in his left shoulder made it feel like Max was putting up a real fight.

He knew he wouldn't be able to climb a tree, but getting the two kids out of sight and behind one of them seemed like something he could do.

When he had accomplished this, he knelt down on the ground and looked Hainey in the eyes.

"Don't go anywhere, okay?"

She nodded.

"And," Jake said, pointing to Max, "don't let him go anywhere either. Alright?"

She nodded again. Though this nod seemed less certain.

"I'm going to try to get Terrance."

Jake stood up and moved back toward the water.

When the stream came into view, Terrance was gone.

And the ripples around the underwater beast were gone too.

He scanned the shore line on both sides of the stream for any sign of either of them.

But neither of them were there.

They had both just disappeared.

5

The water was still.

No bubbles. No ripples. No waves.

No sign of movement whatsoever.

Where had Terrance gone? And what was that thing heading toward them beneath the sludge?

Jake allowed himself to take a moment and survey the stream and riverbanks slowly.

Once he'd determined they were alone, he headed back to Hainey and Max.

"Where's Terrance?" Hainey asked frantically. She was bouncing up and down and her hands were flapping back and forth at the end of her long, dangling arms.

"I don't know," Jake said, trying to compose himself as much as the girl. He knelt down and put his hand on Hainey's shoulder, and met her eyes with his. "But I do know that it's just us for right now. And we're going to be alright."

Hainey looked at him with doubt in her eyes.

Jake understood. If he'd been attached to a lie detector, the man on the other side would have declared him a liar.

He gave a quick look to Max, who was still staring off into space, before standing up and rubbing his chin with his hand.

All he needed was a clue. Something to point him in the right direction.

Jake walked closer to the water.

Everything looked the same. Green and brown everywhere!

Muddy water and trees made it hard to make out anything off in the distance.

When it seemed as though they were stuck, with no direction, Jake spotted something just above the trees.

Smoke?

It was off in the distance, billowing up in a narrow trail before gradually dispersing into a gray cloud and blowing away.

"That's where we're going kids," Jake announced.

"How are we going to get there?" Hainey asked.

A pit of dread dropped into Jake's stomach with a thud at the realization that there was no way they could get to the location of that smoke without crossing the stream.

6

I can do this.

This was Jake's thought as he stared across the murky water.

It isn't that far.

And it wasn't. About thirty feet by Jake's calculations.

But he couldn't manage to shake the thought of the tail of the beast he'd sort of seen. And he couldn't stop thinking about Terrance, and how he'd been there one minute and gone the next.

Had he been eaten by that thing?

Or had he run for cover on the other side?

Or had he gone under, the fear of his impending doom allowing him to swim no more?

Jake had to stop and get all of these thoughts out of his head. He was in charge now. And it was his duty to get Hainey and Max to safety, regardless of how frightened he may have been.

"Do you know how to swim?" he asked Hainey.

She nodded. "My mother…"

Hainey was no doubt about to go into some story about how her mother had taken her to lessons at the local Y, or how her mother had taught her to swim out at her grandpa and grandma's camp, or something like that.

But the thought of her mother was enough to send her into a fit.

"It's okay," Jake said, trying to be compassionate. Though, truth be told, he was feeling the same as Hainey and would've given anything to see his parents again. But someone needed to stay calm.

"We're going to make it out of here," he said.

He left his hand on her shoulder and looked toward Max, whose face was starting to look normal again. The hard, glassy stare he'd had just a few minutes earlier was starting to soften and he was looking around with mild curiosity.

"How about you?" Jake asked. "Do you know how to swim?"

Max stared at the ground and shook his head.

"Okay, no problem. You're going to ride on my back." He turned back to Hainey. "You're going to swim right next to me."

She looked up, scared.

"Don't worry," Jake said, "I'll be right there. Nothing's going to happen to either of you as long as I'm around."

Hainey blinked the tears out of her eyes and nodded. And with a wipe of her face with her arm, she headed toward the water.

7

All three of them had waded in and were standing about knee deep in mucky water.

"Look down," Jake said. "You can't see your feet can you?"

Hainey and Max shook their heads.

"I don't know what's in this water. But remember, whatever's out there can't see our feet either. So just keep moving forward and don't think about anything else."

The kids gave Jake a less than confident nod of understanding.

"Max, climb on," Jake said, kneeling down and allowing Max to climb onto his back and put his arms around his neck.

"Hainey, if you need me for anything, you need to use your voice and tell me. Don't just grab me. Let me know first."

Hainey nodded and the three set out.

They were moving slowly, Hainey taking her cue from Jake, who wanted to be very cautious.

"Nice and easy," he kept saying under his breath.

The water was now up to Jake's shoulders and he knew he would have to start to swim in a matter of seconds. Max wasn't the biggest of kids, but it would certainly be a challenge to stay afloat through the deepest section of the stream.

Hainey was doing well, swimming like a champ right along side Jake. He was impressed with the girl and knew that if they could get all the way across, she would be very helpful along the way.

They were about half way there when Jake felt something squirming around his leg.

He looked over to Hainey, who was actually swimming a few feet in front of him.

Jake decided it would be best to not mention anything to her, and instead allow her to just chug along.

Max also didn't seem to notice anything was going on. He was still and calm as Jake swam.

It was all Jake could do to ignore whatever it was that was beneath the surface. He was thankful that it hadn't grabbed on and pulled.

His feet were kicking and he tried as hard as he could to increase the rate at which he was swimming. But with Max on his back, all of his efforts seemed futile.

A few more feet.

That's all that was left.

Hainey was just starting to climb up onto the bank. She was happy and out of breath.

"I've never swum that far before!" she exclaimed triumphantly.

"That's great!" said Jake, who stayed in the water while Max climbed off of him and up onto the bank.

Max wasn't as enthusiastic as Hainey. He was more relieved that anything. And though he'd done no swimming on his own, he put his hands on his knees and hunched over, sucking wind like he would never breath again.

Jake was just about to stand up and join the two on land when he felt a tug around his left ankle. It was hard and jerked him back down into the water. His full body was submerged now, his face the only part of him above the surface.

"Jake!" Hainey yelled, seeing the fear in Jake's eyes as he went down.

"Stay with Max," Jake yelled back, just before he was dragged under.

8

The panic made the air leave Jake's lungs faster than he'd hoped. He was struggling to get back to the surface to take a breath.

His muscles were beginning to tighten and spasm from lack of oxygen.

If he couldn't find a way to get up to the surface, it wouldn't take long for him to drown.

A searing pain was coursing through his ankle where the beast, or whatever it might be under there, had him.

For a moment he thought of opening his eyes, but he knew that wouldn't help.

Reaching down for his ankle, he grabbed onto the thing that had grabbed him.

He pulled hard and found that the harder he pulled, the harder *it* pulled.

When he let go, *it* let go a little.

Jake knew he was running out of oxygen in his body.

There was only one thing to do if he was going to survive.

He had to surrender and hope that it wasn't too little, too late.

Jake allowed his body to go limp, hoping beyond hope that it would be enough to save his life.

❋ ❋ ❋ ❋ ❋

Hainey and Max looked on in horror as the water thrashed.

Jake had been with them just a moment ago, keeping them safe, helping them to the other side of the stream.

And now.

Hainey had so many thoughts racing through her mind as she watched Jake struggle for his life.

Could she help him?

Should she try to help him, or was it more important for her to take care of Max in the event that Jake didn't come back up?

Would she be able to get herself and Max to that smoke in the distance?

The water continued to move violently back and forth, crashing into itself. She couldn't make out what was happening under there, but she had a feeling it was better that she not know.

Jake's fingers came up momentarily.

She could see them.

And though he was a good seven or eight feet away from the bank, it looked as though he was close enough to reach out and grab.

As soon as they had come up, they had gone back down.

And then the water stopped moving.

9

Jake could feel himself floating.

The tugging on his leg had stopped. The pain was still present, but he could tell that his ankle was no longer being pulled upon and wrenched downward.

There was a tightness and a burning in his chest and throat, his body's way of letting him know that if he didn't take a breath, it would all be over soon.

If he moved too quickly, though, he feared that he would be grabbed and brought down again. And the next time the thing got him, Jake was sure it wouldn't be so quick to let go.

Was he heading toward the bank, where Hainey and Max would be able to grab him and help him up onto the shore?

Or was he sailing down the stream, farther away from them?

Or was he simply laying face down in the water, perfectly still, the lack of air and blood to his brain making it feel as though he was moving?

There was only one way to find out.

He made a move upward and out of the water.

His intention was to make this movement slow and steady, but the subconscious panic in the back of his mind forced him to jerk up and gasp for air.

Jake heard Hainey shriek in the distance.

Once he caught his breath, he would wipe his eyes and try to locate her. But one thing at a time.

The water seemed to be taking him somewhere. With every breath he took, it felt like he was floating forward.

"Jake!" Hainey's voice was farther away than it had been just a moment ago. "Get out of there!"

He brought his hand up out of the dirty water and wiped the sludge from his face.

The flow of the stream had changed and Jake could see the froth of rapid waves crashing into each other. Jagged rocks jutted out of the surface of the water.

At first, he tried to avoid them, but then he looked farther ahead and realized that he was racing toward a waterfall.

He didn't know how far down the drop would take him, but he wasn't about to find out.

10

He flailed his arms and kicked his feet almost uncontrollably. Despite the fact that he was racing toward a drop off the side of a watery cliff, Jake found himself wishing that he would've paid a little more attention during the swim lessons his mother had signed him up for at the local Y a few years back.

He had spent so much time arguing with her about it and telling her that he didn't want to take them, that by the time he was dropped off at the lessons, he often found himself in a sour mood, and spent most of his time brooding in the corner, while the instructors spent their valuable time with the other students; the ones who were interested.

As the cliff got closer, Hainey's voice was drowned out by the rushing of waves colliding with other water particles and rocks.

The speed of the water was taking Jake so quickly he barely had time to think.

He was plunging under for what seemed like minutes at a time, especially with what he'd just been through.

His lungs burned as he crashed through and came up for a quick gasp before heading back below.

It was instincts that saved him in the end.

Nothing more, nothing less.

He was just about to go over the cliff when he reached out his hand, hoping to hit something.

What he hit was a rock.

It hurt.

Stung was more accurate.

He didn't have time to worry about it though. The force of the water was still as strong as ever. If he didn't hold on and ignore the pain, he'd surely go over and find himself on the undesirable side of death.

It happened too quick for him to know exactly what he did or how he'd done it.

But somehow he found himself perched on top of the rock, the water no longer clawing at him.

He was panting like a dog that had just chased a car around a full city block.

As he caught his breath and looked around, it startled him just how close he was to going over the edge.

He could see most of the way down. It had to have been a couple of hundred feet.

Even if it was just water down there, the force of the fall probably would have been enough to kill him.

His left hand and fingers were throbbing. The hand and forearm were covered in blood. It looked pretty bad, but Jake could tell that it looked worse than it was. Water had a way of magnifying and exaggerating the amount of blood on a wound.

He dropped it into the water to get it cleaned off, just so he could see what kind of a wound they were dealing with.

When he brought his hand back up, he saw a cut, about a quarter inch wide and four or five inches long.

It was enough.

But as long as he could keep himself free of infection, it would be little more than a nuisance.

Jake stood up on the rock, trying to keep his balance and get a good look at what he would have to do to get back to Hainey and Max.

He was only about twenty feet away from them.

Hainey was looking around the trees and rooting around in the bushes, trying to find something long enough to hold out to Jake.

And then, as if someone had turned off a switch, the water stopped and several stepping stones emerged.

They were flat and positioned about a foot apart from one another.

It would be easy for Jake to traverse these stones to the river bank.

But could he trust them?

11

Hainey yelled to Jake.

"Did you see that?"

Jake nodded tentatively and asked, "Do you think they'll hold me if I jump across them?"

"It's worth a try. What's the worst thing that could happen?" Hainey shrugged her shoulders.

Max was standing behind her looking flummoxed.

"What do you think Max?" Jake called over, not wanting Max to feel left out.

Max gave Jake a weird scrunchy look, like that of a kid chewing on a lemon for the first time.

Jake took this to mean Max wasn't sure.

"Here goes nothing." Jake took the first step very cautiously, keeping one foot fully planted on the jagged rock he'd caught himself on. His hand was outreached and holding tightly to the highest point of the stone.

When his free foot touched down on the first stepping stone, it sunk and disappeared beneath the water.

Jake removed his foot and the stone bobbed back up.

"Okay," Jake yelled to Hainey. "Stay there. I know how this works. I just have to time it correctly and not stay on any one stone for too long."

Hainey moved her head up and down, her eyes focus intently on Jake's feet.

Jake licked the salt away from his lips and swept his hair out of his eyes with is free hand.

He removed his anchor hand from the rock that had saved his life and prepared to take a few leaps of faith.

He looked up toward the sky and whispered a quick prayer before he took his first step.

It caught him by surprise, just how quickly the stone dipped into the water now that he had let go and disengaged from the first rock.

This was going to have to be quick if he didn't want to fall into the water again.

Jake had never thought of himself as nimble. He could barely swim and sports were something he'd never been interested in.

But in this moment, his body snapped into action and he hopped his way across the remainder of the stream, one falling rock at a time.

When he got to the last rock, whether for dramatic effect, or just because he thought he wasn't going to make it, Jake dove for the patch of grass next to Hainey.

He landed stomach first, his face touching down almost as roughly as their plane had the day before.

"Are you alright?" Hainey asked, rushing to help Jake.

Jake's head popped up, his mouth full of grass in the shape of a smile.

"I couldn't be better."

12

After Jake had taken a moment to brush himself off and spit the remaining bits of dirt and grass from his mouth, he turned and looked at the stepping stones, which had all but disappeared.

He looked further out into the water, surprised to see that where a waterfall had been moments ago, now there was nothing. The stream continued on for as far as he could see, and the jagged pieces of rock that had stuck out and come to his rescue were gone.

"What the heck?" he wondered out loud.

He looked down at Hainey, his palms open and jabbing out toward the water. "You saw it right? I'm not totally crazy am I?"

Hainey nodded.

"I'm crazy? Or you saw it?" Jake asked.

"No, I saw it too," Hainey said, giving Jake the smallest breath of relief.

He turned and walked toward the nearest tree. Once he'd inspected every possible nook and cranny he thought something could stow itself away in, he sat down.

What is this place?

He thought to himself for a moment or two as Hainey and Max joined him at the base of the tree. It would be nice if he could run some ideas past them, but Max, to this point, had been pretty much useless and Hainey, though she was coming out of her shell, was still only five. Jake couldn't hold out hope that she was going remain as assertive and helpful as she'd been thus far.

The pieces floated around in the front of his mind: They had crash landed in a tree; their parents had just disappeared; they were left to fend for themselves in a jungle that seemed to be able to change at will.

Jake craned his neck and looked in the direction where the smoke had been billowing earlier. That was their goal before Terrance had disappeared and the stream had had its way with things.

"Whatever this place is," Jake started, "I don't think we're going to get many answers sitting here for too long. Let's take a few more minutes and then we'll start walking toward that smoke stack. Maybe somebody there has some answers for us."

Max sniveled and gave a whimper. He was crying again.

Hainey put her hand on top of Max's. "It's going to be okay, Max. Jake is going to get us out of here, aren't you Jake?"

Jake didn't know how to respond. It seemed that if there was anyone who would get them out of this mess, it would be Terrance. But he was gone, and Jake was left.

"I'm going to try," Jake said, though he wasn't very sure he could.

13

The walk was relatively uneventful. Aside from the mosquitos landing on them and trying to suck their blood non-stop, and the oppressive humidity that weighed them down like a thick, wet blanket, no other obstacles presented themselves.

There were a few times when Max dropped to the ground and refused to go any further. But a few minutes of Hainey working her magic and he was back up and they were moving again.

Unlike the walk they had taken from the point of the crash to the tree that they called their camp on the first night, this walk was relatively short, only taking them about an hour to get within clear sight of the structure that had the smoke coming from it.

It was basically a hut, made out of grass and dried mud, with a hole in the front that allowed access to the inside.

"Let's stop here for a moment and figure out what we want to do," Jake said, sliding himself behind a tree.

Hainey and Max followed.

"Finally," Max huffed.

"You did a good job Max," Hainey said.

Jake was thankful to have Hainey with them. He knew that if it was up to him to coax Max into moving along, the kid would've been over his shoulder by now, or left behind.

"We're going to stay together and walk up to the hut. You two are going to stay behind me.

Don't say anything. Let me do the talking, okay?"

"I don't want to go!" Max whined. "I'm scared!"

"Well so am I," Jake snapped. "But we all have to do things we don't want to do sometimes."

Jake turned and started to walk toward the hut.

Max continued to argue. "But Jake, I just want to—"

"Zip it!" Jake said, feeling his annoyance with Max starting to bubble over. "You're going to have to do the best you can to suck it up and deal with this, okay?"

Max didn't answer, but the shocked look in his eyes gave Jake the feeling he'd gotten the message loud and clear.

Jake turned and began walking slowly toward the hut.

It was surprisingly open, given the denseness of the rest of the jungle they'd seen along the way.

The hut was located in a large circular area of trampled down grass and mud. Off to one side of the hut was a hand dug fire pit with some sort of animal's leg attached to an unmanned spit.

The bottom of the leg was charred black and the juices were seeping out of the top and running down the sides, dropping into the fire every so often, causing the flames to rise up and envelope the whole of the cooking apparatus.

On the other side of the hut was something that looked like a clothesline. Two thick sticks were stuck into the ground and there was a thin white piece of string connecting them.

But instead of clothes dangling from the strings, there were all different varieties of what looked like teeth. Not human teeth, but something sharper and more primitive; like that of the animal that was now roasting on the other side.

Jake could feel hands grabbing him from behind. Max had nestled up to him on his right side and was squeezing him rather hard around the waist. Hainey was on the other side, though she wasn't outright squeezing Jake. Rather, she had taken hold of his shirt and was twisting it nervously, wrapping it around her thumb and index finger.

He put his arms around both of them and guided them forward.

There was no door on the front of the hut.

As they approached the threshold, Jake called out a tentative, "Hello?"

There was no answer.

"Is there anybody in there?"

Again, no answer.

Jake could feel Max and Hainey's hearts beating fast through the back of their shirts. They were almost beating as fast as his own.

He took one step closer and let go of Max and Hainey, bringing his finger to his lips.

It was now or never. They'd made it this far. He had to look inside and see what or who was in there.

As he put his head inside the hut for the first time, the smell of damp mold was overwhelming. It was almost too dark to see anything past the doorway.

He heard a chuckle in the corner. It sounded familiar.

"Who's there?" Jake called.

"Just me," returned the voice, as Terrance stepped out of the shadows. "What took you so long?"

BOOK THREE

1

Jake eyed Terrance with disbelief.

"We thought you were — "

"Dead?" Terrance laughed. "Lennon, why don't you and the kids come over and have a seat? I have something to tell you."

Hainey and Max were still clinging to Jake. The trust that they had exhibited toward

Terrance earlier had all but disappeared when he had.

And now that he was standing here in front of them, without so much as a scratch, telling them jokes and laughing at their worries, they doubted they could ever trust him again.

There was a wooden bench in the corner. It was made crudely from some tree branches and a flat piece of wood that looked like it had been sliced down the middle by a lightning strike some time ago, and then brought here to be fashioned into a makeshift bench.

Jake took his hand and set it on top of the bench and gave it a quick downward push.

"It'll hold you," Terrance said. "If that's what you're worried about. I know it looks awful, but it's quite comfortable." He motioned them to sit.

Jake took his spot in the middle, Max on his right and Hainey on his left.

The bench wobbled a little bit from side to side, but was sturdy enough.

Terrance walked over to them and stood directly in front of Jake. He stared down and asked, "Do you want to see something cool?"

"I don't think so," Jake said. "I want to see my parents. I want to see my bed. I want to see my home. If you can do that, then that would be *cool*."

Terrance snapped his fingers and a chair emerged from the floor of the hut.

Jake noticed that the chair was not made in the same way as the bench he and kids were sitting upon.

It was more of a throne, made from dark wood that had been meticulously cared for. It was mammoth.

Terrance sat on his throne, which definitely looked as though it should be seating a much larger man than Terrance. He had to sit with his hands on his lap because the giant arms of the throne were even with his shoulders.

"How did you do that?" Jake asked.

"I can do anything, Jake," Terrance replied cooly. "You name it I can do it...so long as I want to."

Jake ran his hand through his hair and blew out a sigh. He was trying to put all of the pieces to this puzzle together. But this puzzle seemed too difficult. Not to mention, this puzzle seemed to have rules all its own; rules Jake hand't yet figured out.

"Why'd you leave us?" Hainey asked, breaking her silence.

"So I could see."

"See what?" Jake jumped in.

Terrance leaned forward in his chair. "If you were worthy of continuing this task."

"And what task would that be?"

"That *task* would be the task I've laid out for you." He jumped down from his chair and walked toward the door of the hut. "Follow me," he ordered.

Jake, Hainey and Max stood up and followed Terrance slowly.

2

The sun was blinding as Jake emerged from the hut. His eyes needed a second to adjust.

"Over here," came Terrance's voice to Jake's right.

Jake turned and followed the voice tentatively. The kids were holding onto his hands tighter than before.

When he could finally see, and only a few sun spots remained in his line of vision, Jake saw Terrance standing next to the clothesline that was near the hut.

Terrance was holding his open palm up toward the line, which had several sharp teeth dangling from it.

"This is my collection," he announced. "I have teeth from every creature in the jungle. Well, actually, allow me to back up. It is my goal to have teeth from every creature from the jungle adorning this line. But at the moment, I'm short three."

Jake looked closely. There had to be forty or fifty teeth all lined up. Some of them were as small as a broken pencil lead, while others were easily the size of his forearm.

"How did you get all of those?" Jake asked.

"Same way I'm going to get the last three," Terrance smiled, "by using kids like you to find them for me."

"Aren't you a kid like us?" Hainey asked.

Terrance laughed. "I'm a kid alright. But not like you."

"Then what are you like?" Jake said, stepping closer.

"I'm going to warn you right now, that if you think you're messing with a kid like yourself, you are sorely mistaken. Now, kindly back up and give me room to speak."

The sudden change in Terrance's voice startled them, and they took a step back.

"Like you," Terrance began, "I ended up in this jungle some time ago. I thought if I just survived for long enough then surely they'd send someone to rescue me. You see, I didn't come upon this place as the result of a plane crash, but rather my parents and I were sailing along the coast during the largest storm these parts have ever seen. They said it was a hurricane and that anyone who didn't have to be in the water or near the coast should head inland for the best shot at survival.

"Well, my parents didn't listen to warnings too well and our boat capsized. At the time, I didn't know what happened to them, but I washed up on the sandy beaches of this place. And once I accepted the fact that my parents were gone, I realized that I would have to survive out here... alone."

Jake put up a hand. "Wait a minute. So you weren't on our plane?"

"No."

"Then how did you get up in the tree with us?"

"That's a good question," Terrance said, shifting his weight off of the clothesline and onto both feet. He folded his arms the way Jake's father always did when he was getting ready to tell Jake some difficult news. "You see, I quickly realized that survival in the jungle for a twelve year old boy is highly unlikely. I gave it a shot. But in the end, the jungle did what the jungle does. Food was difficult to find and getting a clean source of drinking water proved impossible."

"So, what? Are you telling us you died?"

Terrance nodded.

3

Jake could feel himself grow wobbly, Hainey and Max gripping harder than ever, pulling on his shirt. He fell to one knee and looked up at Terrance. "How are you here then? Are we imagining things?"

Terrance shook his head. "This jungle is not what you think it is."

"What is it then?"

"I'm still trying to figure that out myself," Terrance smiled. "Come here, I want to show you something else." He began walking over to the other side of the hut, to where the piece of meat was roasting above the open flames. "Do you know what that is?"

Hainey guessed, "Chicken! My mom used to cook chicken like that when she took me camping."

"That's a good guess," Terrance said, "but it's not chicken."

Jake looked toward Max, wondering if there was any possibility he might wager a guess. Max was in the process of wiping his eyes with Jake's shirt. He was shaking. Jake put his arm around Max and gave him a tight squeeze on his shoulder. "It's okay, we'll make it through this."

Jake looked at Terrance and said, "Listen. We've been through a lot. Can you just tell us what's going on here, so we can try to figure out how to get home?"

He wasn't sure if it was the light from the fire reflecting in Terrance's eyes that gave them such a menacing look, or if something within Terrance had changed. A chill went through Jake's spine, forcing him to shiver. And then Terrance's eyes went back to normal.

"What was that? What just happened?" Jake wondered out loud.

"I just sent you a warning," a smile formed on Terrance's lips. "It's always like this the first time..."

"The first time what?"

"The first time someone new meets me. They always want to control how the conversation goes. Everyone's always in such a hurry to get out of here. Nobody wants to take time anymore and sit down with the resident ghost of the jungle. I mean, think about me for a change, would ya? Do you have any idea what it's like to wake up day after day and wonder if you're going to meet someone new? Do you think it's easy to just sit around by yourself, waiting for a little bit of human contact? I don't even know why I bother any more. You're all the same. Rush, rush, rush. Everyone just wants to get this whole experience over with. They want to go home to their beds and have their parents back and forget about this place; remember it only as the nightmare that it was and tuck it away in their dreams forever. You want this place to be just a small 'blip' on the map of your life. Well, I have news for you kids: This place will haunt you forever."

Jake was starting to really fear Terrance for the first time. Some of the things Terrance had done had been startling and unnerving, but now, something deeper began to present itself. He wasn't quite sure if he believed Terrance was really a ghost. But he was beginning to realize that Terrance might be very dangerous. Jake decided to change his tone quickly to see if he could garner some good will. "What can we do for you?"

"Well, for starters, you can offer a guess as to what this lovely piece of meat used to be." Terrance moved his arm and hand up and down like a game show host showing off a prize to be won.

"You already said it's not chicken, right?" Jake said, playing along.

Terrance nodded.

"And this is not the type of place you'd find a cow, right?"

Terrance nodded and raised a finger. "But, don't get boxed in. There are many things in this jungle that you would never guess were here."

Jake moved a hand up to his chin and began rubbing back and forth. He scrunched his eyebrows together, trying to make it look like he was really giving this a lot of thought. "I don't know, perhaps it's tiger."

"Is that your final guess?"

Jake took one last look at the half charred piece of gristle that was suspended above the flame. "Yes. Yes, I suppose it is my final answer."

Terrance began laughing hysterically and slapping his hand on his thigh. "It's not a tiger or a chicken. No siree. The meat on that spit used to belong to a velociraptor."

"I'm sorry," Jake stammered. "Did you just say *velociraptor*?"

"I sure did Jake."

"You mean to tell me that this place has dinosaurs living in it?"

Terrance smiled and put his hands on his hips. "I told you this jungle wasn't normal."

4

Hainey and Max tried to catch Jake, but it was no use. He was bigger and heavier than either one of them were prepared to handle.

Jake's back hit the ground with a thud, dirt from the ground creating a cloud of smoke around his lithe frame.

"What's wrong with him?" Hainey asked Terrance, and then turned back to Jake. "Jake! Come on Jake, wake up!"

"It's no use," Terrance said. "He's passed out. Most people do that when they hear there are dinosaurs in the jungle. Don't worry, he'll come to in a little while. Help me get him inside."

Terrance bent down and grabbed both of Jake's feet and began to pull.

"He's heavier than he looks," he joked as he rounded the corner through the hut door. He dragged Jake over to the bench they'd sat on earlier.

"I'm going to need your help lifting him up. We're going to put him on this," he pointed to the bench. Pointing at Max, "Grab the arm closest to the bench." And then he pointed at Hainey and ordered her to take the other arm.

When they lifted, Hainey and Max were able to get Jake's head, neck and shoulders off the ground and Terrance could manage his legs and butt. But they couldn't get his back all the way up.

"Alright, put him down," Terrance grunted. They gently set Jake back down on the dirt floor of the hut. "Normally, I like to treat my guests better than this. But this'll have to do for now."

He clapped his hands together, smiling at Hainey and Max. "That raptor's just about done cooking. Who's hungry?"

5

Terrance had taken the spit off the flame and set the raptor leg, charred section face down, on the ground. "Nobody's gonna eat that anyway," he snorted. He stood up and walked back into the hut to get something that he'd forgotten. When he came back the kids were shocked to see him walking with a three foot long sword.

"It's not much of a machete. It used to be a lot sharper, but time and use have rendered the blade dull. And if I wasn't so lazy, I'd have sharpened it by now. But you know, it's no big deal. It still gets the job done…just have to work a little harder on this end."

He brought the blade up above his head and came down hard on the cooked leg. Juices splattered as a chunk fell off the end. The juice was still hot as it hit Hainey's leg. She let out a surprised squeal as the pain registered and she tried to wipe the searing liquid from herself.

"Sorry about that," Terrance said. "I forgot to tell you that you might want to step back. This is going to be pretty hot on the inside."

"Thanks," Hainey said sarcastically.

She and Max each took several steps back, Max grabbing Hainey's arm. They watched, half in horror, half in amazement at what Terrance was doing. When he was finished, he'd cut the leg into sections that looked like that of a watermelon with no seeds. The inside was pinkish red and the outside was a crusted layer of scaly skin.

"I have some bowls inside," Terrance said. "But I find that if you hold it just right, the outer skin has enough structure to keep everything in place."

He handed a small piece to Hainey. "I know you'll have to take the lead on this one, otherwise Max won't even think about eating it." Terrance looked at Max and said, "Trust me buddy, I know it looks repulsive, but starving to death ain't no picnic either."

Hainey and Max didn't want to eat a raptor. They didn't even know what a raptor was. But it looked gross. And smelled grosser.

It was grizzled and tough, like a roast that had been cooked too fast. It didn't really have much of a flavor. At least not one that they could compare to anything they'd eaten before.

They ate just enough to fill their bellies. And neither one of them were convinced that it would stay there for too long.

"Just try not to think about what you've eaten. Go about your business and forget about it until you have to have another go." Terrance smiled as he threw what was left of his section off into the trees. "What do you say we go have a look at Jake and see if he wants any."

Hainey and Max took what was left of their raptor and chucked it toward the trees as Terrance had done. And then they followed him back into the hut as the sun started to disappear below the horizon.

6

Jake was starting to come to. He could hear footsteps shuffling across the dirt floor of the hut. They stopped right next to his head.

"He's still breathing," he heard Terrance say. "A good sign."

Jake could hear Max's sniffles in the darkness, and he could smell something oily. The smell was worse than that. It was burnt. And the closer Terrance came to him, the stronger the smell became.

He tried to open his eyes to see what was going on, but they wouldn't cooperate. They fluttered and stuck together.

"It's okay," he heard Terrance say. "Take your time. You've got nothing but time here."

That was enough to substantially freak Jake out. He popped up off the floor and managed to get his eyes completely open as he stood up. The blood rushing from his head left him momentarily dizzy, and his time spent on the hard, dirt floor had made his back stiff.

He shook his head and rubbed his eyes. Terrance came into focus now. Jake couldn't tell what he hated more: that he was stuck here or that Terrance held the key to him getting home.

"There, there," Terrance said, half mockingly, as he took a step forward and patted Jake gently on the shoulder. "I assure you, Jake, there is absolutely no rush at all. We have eternity if you'd like it."

"What do you need from us?"

Terrance put a finger up to his chin and nodded, looking from Hainey to Max to Jake. "I suppose I've put you three through enough." He turned and went into that dark corner of the hut. Jake could hear him moving objects around, muttering under his breath. "Ah, here it is."

He emerged from the corner with an embarrassed smile on his face. "You know, sometimes it's the most important things that tend to get misplaced the easiest."

In his hand was a rolled up piece of parchment. He walked over to the bench and began to unroll it. He turned to Max and Hainey, "Do you think you two could go outside and find us four rocks? There are some over by the fire. But don't take the ones right around the fire, they'll burn your little hands."

Hainey grabbed Max's hand and they left to retrieve the rocks.

"Now that we're alone, I've got to tell you something," Terrance said leaning in close to Jake. "This task you three are about to go on is dangerous. It's going to be on your shoulders to get those two back into their parents' arms. No pressure or anything."

Jake glanced at Terrance with hatred in his eyes. His jaw line was tight and he could feel his teeth grinding inside his mouth.

Hainey and Max returned, both of them holding two rocks that were slightly larger than a tennis ball.

"Those are perfect," Terrance exclaimed as he began to unroll the parchment. "Just put one in each corner here."

Once the paper was secured, Terrance took a step back and made a motion with his arm in the direction of the bench. "Ta-da!"

"What is it?" Jake asked bitterly.

"I can see you don't share my excitement," Terrance remarked. "Though, to be fair, if I was in your position I doubt I would be very excited, either. It's a map of the jungle."

"That's a map?" Jake laughed. "You can't be serious. How is that a map? It's a circle with three dots and an X."

"Jake," Terrance said, putting his arm around Jake's shoulders. "I like you. And that's why I am telling you right now, just how important it is for your future safety, and the future safety of Max and Hainey, that you shut your mouth and quit being so smug."

Jake looked into Terrance's eyes. The menacing look from earlier had returned. Jake wasn't sure how dangerous Terrance could be, but he knew he didn't want to find out. "Okay," he said. "Sorry about that. What are we supposed to with this map? How're we supposed to use it?"

"That's more like it," Terrance smiled and stepped forward. He pointed at the X. "This is us. Well, not us per se, but our location. This campground. These dots," Terrance said making a semi circle with this finger as he pointed out their locations, "are your destinations."

"And when we reach our *destinations*, what would you like us to do?"

"Funny you should mention that," Terrance smirked. "Follow me."

He walked out of the hut and turned to his right, and stood in front of the clothesline filled with teeth of all shapes and sizes.

"You see those?"

Jake nodded.

"It's quite a collection, ain't it?"

Again, Jake nodded.

"Well, sad thing is," Terrance said, shaking his head dramatically, "it's three teeth short. I have one tooth from every type of animal in this jungle save three."

"So those three dots are the places where those three animals can be found?"

Terrance nodded. "To the best of my knowledge, which at this point is pretty right on." He stopped to flash a creepy grin at the two younger children, who were now, once again, hiding behind Jake. "I can't guarantee that you'll find what you're looking for, but those dots are the places where they tend to hunt."

"Hunt?" Jake asked. "You mean we're going after animals that eat other animals?"

"Well, duh! The animals that eat plants are easy to deal with. They don't really present much of a risk at all."

"So, you're saying that if we go out and get you these last three teeth for your collection then we'll be able to go home and see our families again?"

"Yup."

"And the only animals that you have yet to get teeth from are among the most dangerous animals in that jungle?"

"Yup."

Jake looked at Hainey and Max. He knew he wasn't their father, or even their older brother, but he couldn't help but feel an overwhelming sense of responsibility. "Do I have to take them with me? Or can I leave them here in the safety of your hut?"

Terrance shook his head. "They're part of this. They go with you and either help you obtain the teeth or act as a hinderance."

"Are you going to, at least, tell us which animals we're going to encounter?"

"Nope," Terrance laughed. He looked up toward the sky and noted that the sun was awfully low. "You'd better come in for the night and get a good night's sleep before heading out. Jake, can I interest you in a nibble of raptor meat before you lay down?"

"No."

"Suit yourself," Terrance said before turning back toward the hut and disappearing into its darkness.

"I'm scared, Jake." Max was looking up into Jake's eyes and for the first time since this whole trip began, Jake realized the fear that Max was going through. It now clutched him in the same way. He tried to stay strong, but he could feel the tears forming in his eyes.

"I know, Max." Jake patted him on the back and gave a Hainey a tight squeeze before they entered the hut for what would undoubtedly be a very rough night of sleep.

7

"Come on now! Yer waistin' daylight!"

Terrance's voice boomed and was followed by a bucket of cold water being thrust upon Jake's head.

Jake shot up. "What'd you do that for?"

"I don't want you to miss out on anything," Terrance said smiling. "Have you ever heard the expression, 'the early bird gets the worm'?"

"Yeah."

"Well, according to my calculations," Terrance looked at an imaginary watch on his wrist and then stuck his head out through the door of the hut, "you're very lucky to be the only birds out here."

Hainey and Max were spared the water, but they were starting to wake up as a result of Terrance's loud voice.

Terrance walked over to Jake and handed him the rolled up map from the night before. "Take this with you, but don't lose it. I want to make sure I get it back for the next time I get to meet new people." He smiled.

Jake went to grab the map from Terrance's hand, but the map was pulled away. "Ah, ah, ah. You best take care of this like it's your most prized possession."

Jake was running out of patience for Terrance's nonsense and reached out and took the map away from him.

"Feisty," Terrance commented. "I like it."

"Hainey, Max; it's time to go," Jake said, helping the kids out the door.

As they started to walk away from the hut, the sun was boring down on them. Jake remembered watching a friend of his use a magnifying glass once to intensify the rays of the sun as they hit an ant. He remembered how that ant had fried on the sidewalk right in front of them, and how his friend had gotten such a kick out of it, how he'd laughed and laughed. And how Jake couldn't figure out what was enjoyable about such a horrific thing.

Jake looked at the tree line in the distance. And feeling like the ant beneath the microscope, he would certainly welcome the shade that those trees would provide. But the danger that was sure to come with the relief was making him nervous. Jake had sized the largest tooth that Terrance had collected at almost a foot long. He could only imagine what kinds of animals they were going to encounter on this warped treasure hunt.

As they got closer to the tree line, they could hear the rumbling of the jungle: the sound of leaves rustling back and forth against one another; the birds calling to one another, calls of warning and calls of companionship; and the heavy breathing and mighty roars of animals much too large for a few kids to be hunting down.

These last sounds might have only been in Jake's head, but he knew they would be encountering them soon enough and they scared the whits out of him.

"Do hurry back," Terrance yelled from the door of the hut as the others had just about reached the trees. "It gets so lonely here!"

8

When they'd reached the shade of the trees, Jake sat down at the base of one of them. Hainey and Max joined him.

He began to unroll the map. "Grab a side and hold it open for me, please."

Hainey and Max each grabbed a side and looked on as Jake studied it. He put his finger on the X and traced upward toward one of the dots. Then he looked up and to his slight right. He pointed. "I think if we head off in that direction, we'll be looking at the first animal in a matter of a half hour or less."

They stood up and started to walk, Jake rolled the map back up and slid it into his back pocket. Max's hand was holding onto the same pocket. Poor kid, Jake thought. He could feel Max's fingers trembling as he tried to keep up.

Hainey was holding onto Jake's left hand and, though she wasn't shaking as much as Max, her hand was sweaty and she kept having to let go and wipe her palm on her pant legs.

They'd walked for about fifteen minutes when they came upon their first test.

9

Max froze.

Through the foliage he could make out the shape of ,something very, very large. It was moving like a cat, smooth and fluid, head dipped low. It's tail was raised in the air as if it was trying to gather information.

"Pssst." Jake tried to get Max to look in his direction. He'd found a tree to climb and was pushing Hainey up to a safer vantage.

"Max, get over here!" Hainey whispered harshly.

"Easy, Max," Jake instructed. "Just shuffle over nice and easy."

Max took a slow side step, followed by another, and then another.

The monster in the grass stopped, it's tail moving in the direction of Max. He was being hunted and he knew it.

"Don't stop," Jake said. "Get as close as you can before..."

The beast raised his head above the leaves now and Jake could clearly see that they were dealing with something out of a science text book. This was not a lion or a cheetah. They were staring face to face at something that looked like a saber toothed tiger, an animal that had been extinct for thousands of years. Yesterday, this might have shocked Jake. But today, he understood that normal for this jungle was anything but.

Max was startled and ran toward Jake, his hands and feet pawing away at the tree trunk.

Jake gave him a tremendous push and he climbed up to safety. Jake began to climb himself, his heart racing, pumping hard in his chest. His feet were struggling to find a grip on the tree.

He was going to have to do this another way.

"Stay put you two!" he shouted up to Max and Hainey. They were sitting next to one another on a thicker branch that was hanging several feet above the huge jungle cat.

Jake took a chance and ran to another tree and grabbed onto its thick branch and pulled himself up.

The tiger did not take chase.

That's odd, Jake thought to himself. He couldn't figure out why the animal had allowed him to run safely to another tree without attacking.

And then as he looked a little closer, he got his answer.

10

A tooth, roughly the size of Jake's arm was lying on the ground just behind the saber toothed tiger.

Jake took a closer look at the animal to make sure it had both of its prize worthy teeth. Sure as anything, they were both still there, hanging menacingly from the side of its mouth.

He looked around for any other tigers that may be missing such a tooth.

There were none.

"I see a tooth," Hainey yelled.

"Yeah," Jake replied. "Me too. It looks like he's guarding it. Can you see any other animals from where you are?"

"No. None."

So this is what Terrance had done. He hadn't actually pulled the teeth from the animals or killed anything in the process. The jungle must've planted these teeth as a challenge for those dumb enough — or desperate enough — to take on the task.

Jake scanned the immediate area, trying to see if there were any other threats he and the kids needed to concern themselves with. It was hard to tell given the denseness of the leaves and trees. After a moment or two of squinting, he realized that no matter what, this was going to be a tremendous risk. And a stupid one at that.

He noticed a long green vine wrapped around the tree Hainey and Max were in. It was coiled around their branch, hanging and dangling about five feet above the tiger.

"Hey, do you think you could uncoil that vine enough to feed it down to our friend?"

"I can try," said Hainey as she carefully shifted her body weight and began to pull up on the vine.

Jake knew that given the circumference of the branch Hainey and Max were sitting upon, it wouldn't take much more than one or two times around the branch before that vine was hanging square in front of the saber tooth's snout.

It would be a good test to see how serious the giant cat was about protecting his prize.

Jake thought that if he went for the vine, then maybe he could slip down undetected and grab the tooth before the tiger even knew he was there. Obviously, this was a risk he didn't want to take unless he had to.

Hainey had just about finished her second time around the branch with the vine and was now dropping it down in front of the tiger.

"Good Hainey. Keep it steady and whatever you do, don't hold on too tight."

Hainey nodded and kept allowing the vine to drop little by little.

When it was swinging back and forth in front of the tiger's snout, the tiger, surprisingly enough, did nothing. It just stood there looking straight ahead. Jake couldn't even tell at this point if it even knew they were in the trees above him.

"Alright," Jake ordered. "Pull it back up."

Hainey, with a little help from Max, got the vine back up and piled it up on the branch.

"What now?" Hainey asked.

"I'm not totally sure this will work," Jake said shrugging his shoulders. "But I think it's worth a try. Can you tie a knot?"

"I don't know," Hainey said. "I haven't quite learned how to tie my shoes yet." She pointed to her feet, which were sporting velcro sneakers. Jake's eyes went immediately to Max's feet. He was also wearing velcro.

"The last time you tried," Jake wondered, "how close did you get?"

"Pretty close," Hainey said. "But it was a few days ago."

Jake didn't have a great deal of confidence in this working, but they had to try something. "Alright. Try your best to make a small loop at the end of that vine. Like the size of your wrist. And then tie it off so that it stays."

Hainey gave Jake a quizzical look.

"Just do what I say and then I'll tell you what you're going to do with it."

It took Hainey a few tries. The first time she ended up making a knot in the vine, but no loop. The second time everything just slipped through and undid itself. But on the third time, she got it.

From where he was sitting, Jake could see that there was a loop at the end of the vine. He had doubts about whether or not it would hold, but he couldn't worry himself about that now.

"Okay Hainey. That looks great," he said. "Now, you're going to lower the vine down behind the tiger this time. Do you think you can get it behind him?"

Hainey looked over the edge of the branch. "I think so. I'll have to throw it off the other side."

"That's fine. This time it has to go all the way to the ground."

She nodded and shifted her weight again as she uncoiled the vine one more time around the branch. "I just want to make sure it's long enough," she said.

"Good idea," Jake acknowledged. "When you get it to the ground —"

"I know, I know," Hainey interrupted. "I'm going to try to get the loop around the tooth and then pull it up."

"Very impressive grasshopper," Jake said smiling.

"Grasshopper?"

"Don't worry about it," Jake said. "Something my parents used to make me watch. The point is that you're right."

She nodded.

"You ready?"

"Yup," Hainey said giving a thumb's up.

"Alright," Jake said. "Here goes nothing."

Hainey smiled and began to slowly feed the vine down toward the ground.

11

Jake watched eagerly as Hainey fed the vine down toward the ground. It was getting close and the tiger was none the wiser.

Jake soon realized that getting past the saber tooth was going to be the easy part of this whole operation. Getting the tooth into that little opening in the vine, especially with two five year old kids on the other end of it, was going to be the hard part.

As the vine reached the ground, Jake found himself cringing at Hainey's first efforts. They were nowhere even close to the tooth. In fact, on the second attempt, the vine hit the tiger on the backside. Thankfully, it wasn't a substantial enough smack to alert the animal that anything was wrong. The tiger moved its tail as though it were swatting a mosquito, nothing more.

"Can you get any closer?" Jake asked, trying not to put too much pressure on Hainey.

"Would you like to do it?" she snapped back at him. "Oh, wait a second, you're over in *that* tree, aren't you?"

Jake was shocked at her lip. For a second he allowed his thoughts to drift away from the mission at hand and back to kindergarten. Would he have ever spoken to an older kid that way when he was Hainey's age? He supposed he wouldn't have. But then again, he'd never been put in a position where he was twenty feet above the ground trying to get a two foot long tooth with a vine.

He decided to let it go.

"Good point," he conceded.

Hainey kept working the vine, moving it from side to side. Her eyebrows were furled and her eyes were like daggers, aimed intently on the object they were seeking. Her tongue was sticking out one side of her mouth and she was moving her head back and forth like a kid playing one of those metal claw games at the arcade. Jake hoped the odds of Hainey getting this tooth were better than that of a kid getting a stuffed animal from one of those machines.

But somehow, he knew the odds were far less. If she were able to get the tooth into that loop and then get it back up into the tree with her and Max it would be a miracle.

Jake had to hand it to her. She was a real trooper.

It was on the sixth real try that she actually hooked the point of the fang. But it slipped out as she tried to bring the vine back up.

"I don't know if I can do this, Jake," Hainey said, her voice trembling with frustration.

Jake nodded. He knew what he had to do.

He crossed his hands and rested his head on them. After sending up a quick prayer for safety, he crossed himself and began his climb down to the ground.

12

When he touched the ground, the first thing Jake noticed was how weak his legs felt. They were jellied like cranberry sauce at Thanksgiving.

He was still behind the thick trunk of the tree and out of the sight of the massive tiger. He bent over to pick up a small pebble. If he was going to risk running behind the beast, he had to test the animal's reflexes.

The stone flew through the air and hit the base of the tree Hainey and Max were sitting in.

The saber tooth moved his head quickly in the direction of noise and gave a loud growl.

"What are you doing?" Hainey yelled from above. "Are you crazy? You're going to yourself killed!"

Jake put his finger up to his lips. He needed Hainey and Max to keep their mouths shut or he was dead meat.

If Jake walked around the perimeter of trees that surrounded the tiger, he might be able to sneak around the back without the tiger detecting his presence. He had to be sure not to make a sound, though, or that would be the end for sure. Jake didn't know how keen the mighty animal's sense of smell was, but he really couldn't worry himself that right now.

Dropping to the ground, Jake began crawling from tree to tree as quietly as he could. He popped his head up every few moments to make sure that tiger was still in his place.

Sweat was dripping down his forehead now, running around the edges of his eyes. He knew what came next. If he couldn't get this under control, the sweat would be in his eyes and he'd be fighting a stinging loss of vision.

Quietly as he could, he took his sleeve and wiped the perspiration off his forehead, away from his eyes.

He noticed how badly he stunk and promised himself that if he ever got out of this jungle alive, he'd shower every morning when his mom told him to, no questions asked.

As he got to the tree that was located directly behind the behemoth, Jake's heart was threatening to jump right out of his chest.

He knew he only had one shot at this. The only question he had in his mind was whether he could be fast and quiet at the same time.

He'd know in a matter of seconds.

Jake looked skyward and muttered another prayer under his breath.

And then he made his move.

13

He was crawling on his belly. He knew that if the saber tooth decided it wanted to turn around and check out what it was guarding, or if Jake hit a branch the wrong way and it turned around because it had been alerted by a natural alarm, he'd be dead. From this position there was no way he could possibly get up and out of the way.

So far, so good though.

Jake stole a second to look up to the tree toward Hainey and Max. Both of them were crying, trying to keep their little snivels at bay.

They were probably helping Jake, truth be told. He thought that it was quite possible that the tiger was staring straight ahead, trying to figure out what those little noises were. Meanwhile, Jake was crawling up behind the distracted tiger, who'd only know that something had happened to his precious treasure after it was too late.

At least that's how Jake hoped things were playing out.

A few feet.

That was all that separated Jake from the tooth…and the tiger.

He knew he could reach out and touch the tooth now. All he had to do was put his hand on it and run. But before he could do that, he had to locate a tree to run to. It would have to be a tree that was close by, and also easy to climb. Because if he startled the beast, it would do him no good to get to a tree he couldn't scale.

Just over his left shoulder, he noted a tree that was only about seven or eight feet away. It was tall and gnarled at the base. It looked like there would be plenty of places for his feet and hands to grip.

Fear took hold of Jake as he realized just how close he was to doing something that could cost him his life. Up until now, it had been something he thought about as being in the future. But now the future was potentially here.

He reached his arm out to grab the tooth that was lying on the ground.

And his worst fears came to life. The tiger turned around. Jake heard Hainey scream loudly up in the tree.

Jake was face to face with the creature, its warm breath rushing over him. He swallowed hard.

A low, fierce growl was coming from somewhere deep within this beast.

Jake wondered if he should play dead as he'd done with the other tigers. It had worked then, perhaps it could work now.

No.

It couldn't work now, could it? The creature had already seen that Jake was very much awake and alive — for the moment.

There was really only one thing to do.

He had to get that tooth and then run like the dickens and hope beyond hope that he was fast enough to get away from this thing.

The tiger moved its front paw forward, urging Jake away.

But instead of running away, Jake took a deep breath, reached out his hand and grabbed the tooth.

14

As he wrapped his hand around the two foot long tooth a strange feeling grabbed hold of him.

He could feel his parents with him. He could smell his mother's cooking and he remembered her reading him stories before bed. It was almost as if his father was right there patting him on the top of the head, telling him he'd done well and that he was proud of Jake for being so brave.

It was the strangest sensation. His parents weren't visible and he knew they weren't there. But he could *feel* them. They were there with him, guiding him through this, letting him know that he was on the right track.

"I love you," he found himself exclaiming as he stood up, tooth in hand.

"Well, I love you too," Terrance said, chuckling as he took the tooth from Jake's hand and tied it to the clothesline with the others.

"What just happened?" Jake asked. "One minute I was face to face with a saber toothed tiger, and now I'm here with you? Where are Hainey and Max?"

"Easy there," Terrance said, putting the final touches on the tooth. He took a step back and crossed his arms, admiring his handy work. "It's quite a bit bigger than the others isn't it? I might have to rethink this display, you know. Ah, well. You were saying?"

Jake had a second to take in what was going on and was now more confused than before. He was standing outside of the hut with Terrance, staring at the tooth collection, which had just been added to as a result of his bravery. The fire from the night before had smoldered itself out and a gentle breeze was blowing across his face, cooling him off.

"Where are Hainey and Max?" Jake asked again. "Please tell me they're not still up in that tree."

"They're fine," Terrance said pointing toward the hut. "Go see for yourself."

Jake walked over to the door and peeked inside. Hainey and Max were sound asleep, Hainey on the makeshift bench and Max on the floor, curled up in little balls. Max had his thumb in his smiling mouth and Hainey was mumbling to her mother in her dreams.

Terrance patted Jake on the shoulder and said, "Great job there buddy boy! Really, great stuff. I've been trying to get this one for a while. I could never figure out how to get past that thing. I would have never attempted to go around it. Good thinking. I mean," he said nodding and giving two thumbs up, "really primo thinking."

"I don't understand."

"What don't you understand?"

"What just happened?"

"Well, come on Jake," Terrance scrunched his face. "You're smarter than that. I mean you were there for crying out loud. You outsmarted the tiger, you grabbed the tooth, you gave it to me. That's what I sent you out there for."

"Is that how it works? Is it going to be like that every time?"

Terrance shrugged. "I don't know, Jake. I've been here for years and I'm still trying to figure things out. This place has a way of messing with your mind, know what I mean?"

Jake did know what he meant. And it filled him with dread. If Terrance still didn't know how this place worked, how was Jake supposed to maneuver himself and the children around and get them back to their parents.

Terrance must've noticed a troubled look on Jake's face. "Oh, don't worry," he said. "You'll figure it out. You know, Jake, I think you're much smarter than I am. I wish I'd had you here to help me out before I...well, you know." Terrance closed his eyes and stuck his tongue out as he dropped his head limply on his shoulders, trying to drive the point home.

This made Jake more uncomfortable than he already was. "So, what do we do now?"

"Well, it's getting late. I think we could agree that you and the kids have been through something pretty intense today. Why don't you just plan on hanging here and getting some rest before you head out again. You have two teeth left and then I can let you go."

"Why can't you just let us go now?"

"Because," Terrance said, sticking out his bottom lip in a mocking pout. "That's not how the game is played."

Jake realized he was stuck here until Terrance was willing to let him go. For now, all he could do was go into the hut and join Hainey and Max in catching up on a little rest before heading back into the jungle again.

BOOK FOUR

1

Jake could hear something from his right. It was difficult to pry open his eyes. They were crusted shut from the first real sleep he'd had in days.

Shifting slightly, he pushed himself into a sitting position on the dirt floor of the hut. He looked around for Terrance and noted that he was not inside with them.

Hainey was lying on the makeshift bench of wood, clutching her hands tight to her chest. She was breathing deep, peaceful breaths. Jake thought he might've seen a smile or two come across the girl's lips, but perhaps that was just wishful thinking.

He could only imagine the types of dreams she was having now. Jake hoped they were pleasant and hopeful; dreams of her mother taking her to the park, or to the store to get her new backpack, or tucking her in at night and gently brushing aside a wayward strand of hair. Or, perhaps, it wasn't even a dream about something that had happened. Maybe it was a dream about the meeting that Hainey and her mother would soon be having just as soon as she was finished hunting for teeth in this God forsaken jungle.

A mumble of sorts that sounded more like a scream broke Jake's concentration. He looked to his right where Max had been trying to sleep. His eyes were closed and he was lying down, but it was hard to define what he was doing as sleep.

His dreams were clearly nothing like Hainey's. There was no happiness inside his head, nothing to comfort him in here on the ground. He began rocking back and forth and Jake noticed tears coming from the boy's eyes, though they never opened.

"Mornin' twinkle toes," Terrance joked, storming into the hut and diverting Jake's attention. "You'd better get these two rug rats up you're going to be way behind."

Jake stood up and brushed himself off. "Way behind what?"

"Your goal," Terrance smiled.

"I thought our goal was to get you the three teeth you were lacking. I didn't realize there was a time frame on the task."

Terrance stopped and thought for a moment. He put his hands together in the shape of a tent and brought them up to this face. It was clear to Jake that he wanted to be very careful with what he was about to say.

"There's not a timeframe per se. But, you should be aware that the more time passes, the more difficult each tooth is going to be to retrieve."

"And why is that?"

Terrance stared at Jake for a moment. The hard eyes Jake had seen the day before came back, almost as though Terrance was trying to intimidate him into getting Hainey and Max up and going without a second thought. But Jake questioned everything. And Terrance's eyes weren't enough to scare him anymore. Not after this place.

"Alright, you got me," Terrance laughed as he softened his eyes and allowed his shoulders to fall. "It's not really going to get any harder. I'm just getting antsy. And I thought you'd be just as eager to see your parents as I am to see mine."

"I am," replied Jake. "But I think it's probably best to go into this with a little bit of rest. And so long as those two are sleeping, I'm going to let them."

"It's okay, Jake. You don't have to go getting all upset about things. Jeez." Terrance smiled and walked back outside.

He strolled over to the clothesline and folded his arms in front of his chest, admiring his collection.

"I didn't think the day would ever come when I was just two teeth short. I thought for sure I'd be here in this jungle forever. But now, thanks to you and Hainey, I'm almost free."

"Don't forget Max," Jake asserted.

"Oh, yeah," Terrance stammered. "Well, let's face it Jake. He doesn't really do much of anything except for whimper and snivel, now does he?"

Jake could feel an anger bubbling within him. He wanted to tell Terrance that he was wrong. He wanted to stick up for Max and tell Terrance about all of the virtuous qualities he saw in the boy. But the truth was, he couldn't. It seemed, for the time being anyway, that Terrance was completely correct about Max.

"I'm sure he'll do something great before this whole nightmare's over," Jake finally said.

"You know the next tooth is actually going to be much smaller than this saber tooth, right?"

"What do you mean?" Jake asked. "They're supposed to get bigger as they go on aren't they?"

"The challenge."

"What's that?"

"The challenge gets bigger. Not necessarily the tooth."

Jake stood back and looked at the row of teeth. It appeared, as his eyes moved across the line, that the teeth were getting bigger. And they were. Certainly, as the line of teeth moved left to right, they increased in size. But not every tooth was bigger than the one before it. It was subtle, but true.

"So, do you know which animal we're going to be attempting to slay next?" Jake asked.

"Yup."

Jake waited, anticipating and answer that didn't come.

"Well?"

Terrance turned, giving Jake an ominous look.

"Velociraptor."

2

Before Jake had too much time to dwell on things Hainey was coming through the door of the hut rubbing her eyes. She stopped briefly and stretched her arms above her head with her back arched, a huge yawn escaping her spittle covered mouth.

"Morning sleepy head," Terrance said cheerfully.

"Morning," Hainey replied in a voice that said, *I'm still way too tired to be awake.*

"What do you say, we go get Max up and enjoy ourselves a good old fashion breakfast," Terrance suggested.

Hainey had a repulsed look on her face.

"Oh, no worries Hainey," Terrance smiled. "It's not going to be anything like the last meal we shared together.   Let me show you what I mean."

He led Jake and Hainey around the back of the hut, where, unbeknownst to anyone but Terrance, there was a chicken coup. It was a few feet wide and a few feet long with two levels. It was made in a makeshift manner, with wire fencing and a few pieces of plywood to separate the top level from the bottom. There were six hens inside, three on the top and three on the bottom.

Terrance walked over and put his hand through an enlarged hole in the fencing. Gently nudging one of the hens on the rear, he reached into a small amount of hay the bird had been sitting on.

Jake and Hainey couldn't see what he was doing, but when his hand came back through the fence, he was holding onto three small, brown eggs.

"It's been a few days since I've collected," Terrance said. "There should be plenty for us to have a great, big breakfast."

Jake smiled with relief that he was going to have something normal, something he was accustomed to before they'd landed in this jungle.

Hainey took off back toward the hut yelling, "Max, wake up! Wake up! Terrance is going to make us eggs for breakfast!"

"Kids," Terrance smirked.

"Yeah...kids."

When Hainey came back she was out of breath but jumping around almost uncontrollably, a fact that the hens seemed to find less than enjoyable.

Max, on the other hand, looked like the breaking of a long winter. His hair was disheveled and he was walking with his head down. It was unclear to the others whether his eyes were actually open while he walked.

Terrance quickly and expertly started a fire with a few sticks and dry leaves. While the fire was growing to good cooking size, Terrance went inside the hut and emerged with a flat metal surface that he'd fashioned to some metal legs.

Jake thought it might've been a table for them to eat their breakfast on, but when Terrance put it over the fire, he realized that couldn't be so.

"Found the pieces to build this baby washed up on shore a few months ago. I know it looks rough, but it serves as a great little hibachi."

"Hibachi?" Hainey asked.

"Yeah. You know," said Terrance, "one of those Japanese style grills. You ever been to one of those?"

Hainey shook her head.

"Well, when you get back to your mother, you be sure to tell her that she's just got to take you, okay?"

Hainey nodded.

Terrace had collected eighteen eggs total and they were now sitting at his feet in the dirt. After a couple of minutes he announced, "I think it's hot enough now."

He picked up two eggs and at a time and began cracking them on the side of the 'hibachi' and dropping the contents onto the flat surface. They sizzled and instantly started to turn white.

"This happens pretty quick. Stay here, but don't touch anything."

Terrance ran into the hut and emerged with four bowls that he'd made from tree bark and a makeshift spoon/spatula that he'd shaped out of some driftwood. He put the spoon in the middle of all the eggs and just started to whip them into a frenzy.

"My mother used to make me eggs all the time," Jake said. "I used to love this part, when she'd scramble them and the dark yellow yolk would meet with the whites and the whole thing would turn into this pale yellow pile of yumminess."

He smiled at that thought.

Terrance said, "We're just about there."

He used the spoon to separate the eggs into four piles and then he slid each pile to the edge and dumped them into a bowl that he was holding just below the edge of the cooking surface.

Once everybody had their bowl of eggs, Terrance smiled an embarrassed smile. "Sorry to say guys, I don't have any forks. You're going to have to use your fingers."

That was not a problem.

Hainey and Max were halfway through their eggs before they'd even found a dry spot of dirt to sit down upon. Wide smiles came across their faces for the first time since before they got on the plane.

It wasn't much, Jake thought, but sometimes all you need is a bowl of scrambled eggs to make you feel at home.

3

After breakfast, with bellies full and hearts warmed, it was time for Jake, Max and Hainey to head out and retrieve the second tooth.

As they stepped away from the safe haven of the hut, the warm thoughts they'd been sharing quickly faded and ran away. They were replaced with the feeling that had flanked them this entire journey — fear.

"Jake?" Hainey asked.

"Yes."

"What kind of tooth do we have to get?"

"I'd rather not say."

"Do you know?" Hainey eyed Jake suspiciously.

"Yes, I do," Jake said.

"Why won't you tell us?"

Jake stopped and thought for a minute. He looked long and hard at Max and Hainey. Of course, he was trying to protect them, to keep them wrapped up in a warm blanket as long as he could. The last thing he wanted to do was freak them out before they were anywhere near their destination.

But what if not telling them was somehow worse? What if he was setting them up for a situation they couldn't handle by not allowing them time to prepare themselves?

He crouched to a knee and unrolled the map, motioning for Max and Hainey to gather around.

"Do you see this," he said, pointing at the dot that was directly east of the hut.

They both nodded, their eyes focused and serious, jaws tense, knowing that they were going be let in on something very big.

"That's our destination," Jake continued. "When we get there, we will be encountering our most dangerous challenge yet. You have to promise me that you will follow me and do exactly as I say."

Again, they nodded.

"The tooth we are in search of belongs to a dinosaur called Velociraptor. When I was in third grade I did a report on these dinosaurs. They're scary. And I thought that when I knew they were extinct. Now that we have one in this jungle, walking among us, I'm petrified."

"What's so scary about them?" Hainey asked.

Max was sitting quietly, shaking slightly.

"Well, for one, they're carnivores, which means they eat only meat. And worse than that, they're hunters, killers. They have sharp teeth and sharper claws. Now, they aren't the biggest of dinosaurs, but they're bigger than all of us. And fast. They can run as fast as a cheetah. So it's imperative that we handle this with a little bit of care."

"So, what's the plan?" Hainey pressed.

Jake looked into the sky and noticed some rather large birdlike creatures circling around them overhead. That's odd, he thought, birds don't usually circle unless they're planning to eat something. And then he took a closer look and noticed that these weren't birds, but rather something a little more prehistoric.

They had massive, leathery wings, which resembled that of a bat's. But the giveaway that these creatures were not birds, was their faces. They didn't have beaks like Jake had ever seen. Rather, they looked to have a long bone ending in a point at the mouth, and extending past the back of the head where it was capped off in a dull curvature.

"Hainey, Max," he whispered. "We need to get ready to run."

"Why?" Hainey asked.

Max swallowed hard and pointed into the sky. Hainey looked up. "What are those?"

"They appear to be pterodactyls," Jake said. "Flying dinosaurs. And it appears they are circling over us, which means it's only a matter of time before one of them breaks rank and comes down to grab one of us."

No sooner had Jake said this that one of the dactyls broke free of the circle and came swooping down toward them. The others took note and began flying in the direction of the ground.

"Run!" Jake commanded.

4

Jake had to be careful as he was running for his life. He had to balance the idea of saving his own hide, with that of his responsibility to keep Max and Hainey safe.

He was sure to keep them in front of him, but the fact that they ran like a couple of five year olds made him nervous. It was fighting instinct not to just turn on the jets and get past them. But if anything were to happen to them, he'd never forgive himself.

As they approached the tree line, most of the pterodactyls decided it wasn't worth it and recognized their own limitations. However, one stingy dactyl continued to follow them, flying below the bulk of the branches.

Leaves, twigs and vines slapped against Jake's body as he ran. His arms and legs took the brunt of it, but occasionally, a low hanging branch would catch him in the side of the face.

He'd wince, but he couldn't stop.

Max and Hainey were running quite fast for their ages. Jake had to admit, he was impressed.

Lungs burning, Jake ventured a look back. The dactyl was slowing down, and the deeper they went the harder it became for it to move its massive wings. Eventually, it just stopped flying and dropped down to the jungle floor.

It stopped moving altogether, looking around curiously, trying to figure out its next move. It looked up to the sky and began calling loudly to the others.

Jake and the kids had taken up hiding behind a thicket of bushes and were now watching in horror as the calls of the dactyl did not have the effect that it'd been hoping for.

A few familiar 'friends' began to emerge from hiding. They were not the pterodactyl's allies.

Three tigers walked cautiously toward the beast and began circling.

The dactyl began crying out now, almost frantically, seemingly hoping that one of his friends would come rescue him. Jake looked up to the sky, and though it was hard to see through the trees, he could make out a few pterodactyls flying helplessly above, looking down on their brother, who was about to meet his maker.

Without so much as a warning snarl, the tigers pounced. Unlike with the snake they'd taken care of earlier, there was seemingly no strategy to this kill. They simply pounced and took whatever pieces of flesh they could.

The dactyl cried out but only for a moment.

Then it was done.

Jake looked up to the sky, and where the other dactyls had been just a moment ago there was only blue sky.

5

Jake tapped Hainey and Max on the back and gave a quiet signal that they need to get going. He put his finger to his lips, warning them to be as quiet as possible.

Hainey nodded and began moving slowly. Max had glazed over eyes, like he'd gone into shock again, but he was able to move and keep up, so Jake didn't worry too much.

It took them a few tense moments to get out view of the tigers.

As they continued, Jake began to realize that they would have to go much deeper into the jungle to retrieve this tooth than they had yet been.

As they moved further into the foliage, it started to become darker and as they continued this way, Jake knew it would eventually become so dark that they would hardly be able to see each other. They were going to have to stop for a minute and get a game plan together, so they all knew what they were going to do when the situation got really dangerous.

Jake reached out to put a hand on Max, who jumped and then dropped to the ground, cowering in fear.

"It's okay," Jake whispered. "It was just me. I was just checking to make sure you were still with me."

"I'm scared, Jake," Max returned.

Hainey laughed a little, but Jake could tell by the tentative shake in her voice, that Hainey was feeling a lot like Max and just showing it in a different way.

"Listen," Jake said. "I'm scared too. But we will get through this. I promise. I'm going to do whatever I have to do to keep us all safe. Do you understand?"

"Yes," Hainey whispered.

"Yes," Max whispered.

"We need to stop for a minute and get a plan together so we aren't too panicked when things start happening. We don't want it to be like last time. We have to admit that we got lucky with the saber tooth. If we do the same thing with the raptor, I think it's safe to assume that we won't be so fortunate."

He took the map from his back pocket and unrolled it again. He pointed to an imaginary area between the marking for the hut and the dot to the left of the hut.

"This is roughly where we are. I think we're getting close to the raptor, but honestly, with us having to run from the pterodactyl, it's made it difficult to gauge our distance. We might be much closer for all I know.

"I think it's a given that we are going to be entering much darker surroundings than these." Jake pointed around, making a circle with his right hand. He then pointed forward, "As we go deeper into these trees, it's going to get very difficult, if not impossible, for us to see where we're going. It may even be hard to see your own shoes."

Hainey nodded impatiently. "Okay, so what's the plan?"

"Yeah," Max piped up.

Jake was taken by surprise, and relieved to see that the kids were just as dedicated to the locating and retrieving of the teeth as he was. It was nice to know that he wasn't just dragging along dead weight through all of this. They would be of some use moving forward, so long as they were able to get on the same page and stay on the same page.

"Understand that all I know of raptors is what I've seen in movies and read in books. But from what I've been able to gather, they are very aggressive hunters. That means they'll be more than ready to sink their teeth into one of us."

Jake notice that Max had started shaking noticeably. He put his hands on Max's shoulders. "Remember what I said, buddy. I'm not going to let anything happen to you if I can help it."

That helped Max a little, but Jake could tell, whether Max wanted to contribute or not, the kid was scared to death. Hainey on the other hand was staring hard at Jake, ignoring Max as best she could.

"So, it's going to hunt us?" she said. "What do we do about that?"

"I was thinking that the best way to hunt something that wants to hunt is to set a trap. The raptor's going to be looking for one of us, possibly all of us. What we have to do is make ourselves as easy to get to as possible."

"I don't follow," Hainey interrupted. "Are you saying that we just let that thing have one of us?"

"Yes, but not really," Jake said raising a finger, hoping to emphasize the brilliance of his plan. "You see, if he comes after one of us, that'll leave two of us left to go after the tooth. Do you remember what happened last time I grabbed a tooth?"

"Oh, I get it!" Hainey exclaimed. "Which ever one of us is not being charged by the raptor is going to haul booty and get the tooth. That way all of us end up back at the hut in one piece and the raptor wanders around hungry. Jake that's brilliant!"

Jake smiled, rolled up the map and stood up. He put his hand on Max's back and gave Hainey a high five.

"Let's go do this," he said trying not to seem too confident.

6

As Jake had predicted, it only got darker as they moved further and further inland. He decided it would be best if they held hands as they walked, so that they always knew where each other was.

Hainey's hands were cool to the touch. The girl had ice water in her veins and it was clear by the way she responded to Jake's plan that she was going to be fine.

Max, on the other hand, was not giving Jake a warm fuzzy feeling heading into this. His palm was soaked with sweat and his grip was completely limp, giving Jake the feeling of holding a saturated wash cloth. Every time he looked down at Max, he swore that Max was looking more frightened than he had the time before. At this rate, Jake was thinking that the only way they were going to be able to get this tooth out from under the raptor's watch was if the beast attacked Max.

Jake was pretty sure that Max could play that part a lot better than he'd be able to be the one of them to run after the tooth if the raptor attacked Jake or Hainey. Either way, Jake was sure that Max would clam up and freeze.

It had turned out to be a much longer walk than Jake had anticipated. The three were tired, hungry, thirsty and just plain out of breath when Jake noticed the thing they'd been looking for in the distance.

He stopped and the others did as well, once they noticed the tug that Jake gave each one of their hands.

"Do you see that?" he whispered.

"Yes," they whispered.

Straight ahead of them in the dark, was a light blue glow. They were about half a football field away and it was hard to make out the actual form of the tooth inside the glow, but Jake knew what it was.

And, just as if on cue, a dark, six foot shadow of a menacing creature moved in front of the glow, blocking it from their view momentarily.

"You guys ready?" Jake checked.

"You betcha!" Hainey chirped.

Max didn't give an answer, but the increased sweat in his palm told Jake that it was now or never.

7

They inched closer, together, hands locked.
One step at a time.

Jake's heart was pounding hard inside his
chest. His breathing quickened, becoming short
and shallow. He could feel Hainey on his right,
moving at a steady pace, holding tight. Max was
on the left and had to be dragged slightly, his
hand like a dead fish in Jake's.

As they approached, they could hear the raptor breathing. It was loud, and for the moment anyway, the dinosaur sounded like a large house cat, purring as it guarded the tooth.

For the moment, Jake thought that the raptor hadn't sensed their presence. But this thought was fleeting and wrong.

As the three stepped closer, the raptor stood up high on its legs, stretching tall and bellowing a call that sounded like a loud cough into the air.

For the first time since he saw Hainey on the plane, Jake could feel her recoil. She was scared and showing it.

Jake tugged on her hand, letting her know that he was there.

They moved forward a little slower, but still pressed the beast.

Again, the raptor stood tall and barked.

In the glowing light, Jake could make out the shadows of trees surrounding the tooth and he let go of Max's hand. Pointing to a tree on his left, he motioned to Max to go in that direction.

Max shook his head fervently, searching for Jake's arm. Once he located it, he gripped it hard with both hands.

Jake didn't want to, but Max was leaving him no other choice. Letting go of Hainey's hand, Jake used his free hand to give Max a swat on the back of the head.

When Max looked up in surprise, Jake grabbed his face with his free hand.

"Get over there," Jake mouthed, making sure he didn't make any more noise than he needed to.

Max let go, looking at Jake like a puppy who'd just been smacked with a newspaper for peeing on the carpet. His trust had been damaged and he would need some time to rebuild it.

Jake was sure that under normal circumstances he might have been bothered by this. But there was no time to worry about feelings now. The only thing on Jake's mind was getting that tooth and getting out of here — alive.

When he turned back to Hainey, he found that she was already in place, standing in front of a tree to the right. She really was reliable. Jake liked her moxie.

As Jake was getting ready to slip in front of a tree directly in front of the raptor, the six foot tall dino reared up on its hind quarters again, and gave one final howl.

There was a moment of confusion, and then Jake's worst fears came true as another raptor came to join the party.

8

The two beasts stood there, side by side, blocking the glow of the tooth, daring the kids to take a step forward and challenge them.

The raptors looked at each other and made a series of clicking noises and hisses, that Jake could only guess were some form of communication.

Finally, one of them started to move slowly in Max's direction. The other one, however, stayed put in front of the tooth.

This wasn't good. Jake had to come up with another plan, and quick, or they'd be going back to the hut minus one. Or worse, none of them would make it back at all.

"Change of plans Hainey," Jake called, a little louder than he'd meant. But it was apparent that the raptors already knew they were there. No need to whisper anymore.

"Ok, what's that?" Hainey called back.

"One of them's heading over to Max right now. I'm going to charge the one that's still in front of the tooth. You need to charge from the other side and just grab that thing."

No answer.

"Do you understand?"

No answer.

"Hainey, are you there?"

"In just nodded yes two times, jeez," she fired back.

Jake marveled for a brief moment at the mind of a five year old. Even a five year old like

Hainey, who seemed so far ahead of other kids Jake had met. He smiled for a second before giving the command.

"Go!"

Out of the corner of his eye, Jake saw the other raptor start running at Max. And then he heard Max scream a blood curdling scream. Jake wasn't sure if Max had been injured, or if he'd taken off running and hidden, but he couldn't worry about that now.

He started running directly at the raptor who was still in front of the tooth. And then he heard Hainey's feet moving as fast as they could across the ground.

In the darkness, it was hard to see how close he was to the raptor, but he knew he couldn't have too much farther to go. At this point, Jake knew he was going to get cut, or bitten. He just hoped it wouldn't be too bad before Hainey grabbed the tooth and they were brought back to the hut to regroup.

As this thought passed through his consciousness, Jake ran into the raptor and fell hard to the ground. And then he could feel the sharp searing pain of a claw pressing against his leg.

9

"Ooowwwww!"

Max's screams filled the air. "Oh my God! Oh my God! Stop it! It hurts so much! Mommy!"

The searing pain in Jake's leg started to subside and as he opened his eyes, he could make out the figures of Terrance and Hainey helping Max onto the bench inside the hut.

"You're going to be okay," Terrance said. "That's right, grab my hand buddy. It'll be okay. Nothing to worry about."

Max rocked from side to side, writhing in pain as Hainey approached with a large leaf and began wrapping it around Max's left arm.

Jake also noticed a scrape across Max's forehead. It was scabbed over and appeared to be healing. Before Hainey could finish the wrap around Max's arm, it was soaked through with blood.

"Get that belt over there," Terrance commanded.

Hainey retrieved the belt and Terrance began wrapping it around Max's bicep.

"This is going to hurt just a little, but it'll be worth it."

Max nodded and then winced and then passed out.

"Oh no!" Hainey cried. "Is he okay? He's not dead is he?"

"No," Terrance assured her, "he's not dead and he's going to be fine...eventually."

Hainey dropped to the ground and began to sob.

Jake wanted to console her. As he stood up, he noticed that his leg was also bleeding, and he had a noticeable limp. He walked, dragging his right leg slightly behind him and then sat down next to Hainey.

He put his arm around the girl. "He's going to be fine."

"It's all my fault," she cried.

"No, nothing here is your fault."

"Yes it is too. If I'd have gotten there faster he'd have never gotten hurt."

"I'm not so sure about that," Jake said. "I heard him scream pretty early on. I don't think there was anything either of us could've done to stop that second raptor from getting to him."

"Second raptor?" Terrance asked. "That's not good."

"What's not good?" Jake asked.

"The jungle is changing. The rules have always seemed to be one tooth, one animal." He walked to the door of the hut, raptor tooth in hand. He grabbed a piece of wire and started to wrap it around the tooth. "Unless, the game is adjusting to you."

"What do you mean?"

"Before, it was just me. So, there was only a need for one animal to guard the tooth because it was only guarding against one person. But, since you guys started going out for the last couple of teeth, the jungle must've changed its strategy or something." He nodded, clearly pleased with his powers of deductive reasoning.

"So what happens now that we're back down to two?"

"Two?" Terrance said, looking at Jake like he didn't understand.

"Yeah, me and Hainey," Jake explained.

"Oh dear," Terrance said, bringing a finger up to his lips. "This presents a problem."

"What kind of problem?"

"It's one, I'm afraid, that is going to put this whole quest in jeopardy."

10

Terrance motioned Jake and Hainey out of the hut.

He began hanging the raptor tooth in its rightful place at the end of the clothesline.

"One more," Terrance said, shaking his head. "You know, it figures. It's always when you're closest to getting where you want to get that life throws in a curve ball to take you off the scent."

"What's that supposed to mean?" Jake asked, trying to hide his agitation.

"I'm not a hundred percent certain, but I think Max has to go with you to get the last tooth or he may not be able to make it home."

"What are you talking about? Who made up that rule?"

Terrance shrugged and then held his hands up toward the sky, as if to say, 'someone out there.'

"That's a bunch of crap," Jake said. He could feel himself starting to come unhinged. "You know what, it doesn't matter. There's no way he's going be able to go back out with us. He needs serious medical attention and you need your last tooth. It seems to me the only way for those two things to happen is for me and Hainey to go back out and get you what you need so that Max can get what he needs…and so we can all get home."

Terrance nodded. "Oh, I totally agree. The problem is, that's not up to me."

"What do you mean it's not up to you? You've been running this whole game from the time we got here. I mean, heck, you even lied to me the first time we met, saying that you didn't know

231

much about this place or whatever it was you said. And then, later we find out that you know everything about this place. So much so, that you've set up this elaborate game of cat and mouse with the teeth of jungle animals. Don't stand here and try to tell me that it's not up to you, because that's a lie and you know it."

Terrance shook his head and kicked his foot through the grass in a sideways motion. "I wish that were the case. But let me ask you this Jake: How do you explain the fact that I'm still here? Huh? I've been here for fifty years, just waiting for the next plane to fly over and crash, or the next boat to capsize and have its occupants wash up on shore. Don't you think, that if I could for one second, figure a way to get myself out of this place, that I might just do that? What? Do you think I enjoy sending you out to the jungle to do what you've been doing? You think I like scavenging for any spare scrap of meat I can find to cook over my fire?"

This stung Jake and made him feel like he'd been wrong about Terrance the whole time. Was Terrance just like them? Had he wanted to go home all this time too? Of course, it made sense now. Terrance's fate was dependent on the fate of others. And if that were the case, then Terrance had the least control over his future of any of them.

"You're right," Jake said. "I'm sorry. But the truth remains, Max is in no shape to go with us. He's going to have to stay here. Hainey and I are going to go and take our chances and let things happen the way they need to happen."

"Okay," Terrance said, looking down at the ground. "Suit yourselves."

"I think we will," Jake said. "Now, if you could kindly tell us which tooth we are responsible for bringing back so that we can get on with it and get out of here, that would be terrific."

Terrance looked up, dark shadows under his eyes. "I'd rather not."

"Come on, Terrance. At least give us some idea of what we're going up against."

He shook his head and began walking back to the hut. "I'm going to check on Max."

"Why won't you tell us?"

Terrance didn't respond. He just shook his head and walked into the hut, leaving Hainey and Jake outside in more ways than one.

BOOK FIVE

1

They'd walked south for hours, stopping every so often to check the map for distance. Based on the distance of this dot from the hut, it would take them longer to find this tooth than any of the others. The map was not to scale, which made it extremely difficult and frightening to continue to walk into the unknown without so much as a head's up as to when something might pop out at them.

Thus far they'd been lucky. The walk had been quiet and slow going. It was almost as though this jungle knew exactly what Jake and Hainey needed at this part of the journey. There were even a few times when a nice gentle breeze found its way to them, moving gently through their hair and across their sweat covered faces. The sensation of relief was short lived, though they were grateful for its presence when they received it.

Jake had thought a great deal about Terrance and Max as they walked. The way Terrance had reacted, it was like they were in a lose-lose situation. The disappointed way he walked away from them, the notion that keeping Max with him would hurt all of their chances, and the idea that Terrance was desperately waiting for someone to save *him* gripped Jake's mind. He couldn't let go of these thoughts as he and Hainey made their way south.

"Jake?" Hainey asked, breaking the silence.

"Yes?"

"What do you think Terrance meant when he said, 'suit yourself?'"

"Not sure."

"Do you think it...I mean...Could it mean that we're not going to be able do this?"

"I don't know, Hainey. I wish I could tell you for sure what he meant. I've been thinking about it a lot myself, and it doesn't make a lot of sense. But it does certainly point in a direction that's not favorable to us."

"Yeah..." Hainey's voice trailed off. "That's what I was thinking too."

"But," Jake said, trying to keep his spirits high as much as hers, "it doesn't mean that we stop what we're trying to do. If we give up then we're definitely stuck here and everything is for nothing. But if we continue on the path we're on, at least we give ourselves a chance."

Hainey nodded, but Jake watched her shoulders slump and she started walking slower. He knew he was in danger of losing her. He just hoped it was after they'd obtained the last tooth. They still had a chance. And that was enough for Jake to keep going.

2

"It's awfully quiet," Hainey said after a few moments.

"I agree," Jake said. "It's like the calm before the storm."

"Huh?"

"Nothing," Jake said. He smirked a little, and thought that Hainey, though wise and brave beyond her years, was still a five year old. That expression must've seemed like a foreign language to her, much the same way it was to him before his father had taken some time last year and explained it to him so that he could finish a reading assignment for school.

Jake was brought back to the present when his foot caught on something on the path. At first, Jake had thought it was just a gnarled tree branch. He turned around and gave a look toward the ground.

Jake picked the object he'd tripped over up and studied it. The two foot long object was heavier than Jake had anticipated. It looked as though it had once been white, but now it was a covered in dirt and looked more gray. His eyes were drawn to the end of the object, where Jake noticed that it looked an awful lot like the bones he'd seen in museums.

"I think this is a bone," he told Hainey. "Let's start looking around for others. They could be a sign that we're getting closer.

A few feet away from the bone he'd tripped over, Jake found a rib cage. He figured it must've been there for a while because all of the meat had been stripped away and some of the bones had broken off and fallen to ground.

"Are you ready? Because I think we're getting closer."

Hainey nodded and started walking upright again, getting herself ready for whatever challenge was ahead of them.

As they continued to walk, the bones began to pile up. Both sides of the path were soon adorned with bones of all shapes and sizes.

The more they walked, the more meat the bones had on them. They noticed an increase in insect activity, mostly flies. They buzzed around the decaying carcasses of whatever animal it was that had been unceremoniously left in the brush for dead.

A breezed kicked up, blowing foul air with it from the south. The stench of day old death hung in the air and started working hard on Hainey. She couldn't help herself and threw up in the bushes. Morning eggs and bile now joined a half covered skull fragment.

The eyes of the dead animal stared up at Hainey, forcing a shudder and then more eggs.

"You okay?" Jake asked, putting his hand on her back, more to let her know that he was there if she needed any help.

She emerged wiping her mouth with one hand and her eyes with the other before she collapsed into Jake's arms.

"I want to go home," she cried. "I just want to see my mommy again. I don't want to be here anymore, Jake. I'm scared."

Jake held her tight, trying not to breath through his nose. "I know Hainey. We're almost there."

After a few moments, Jake tentatively let go of Hainey and they stood looking at each other in the midst of the rot. He nodded at her and she returned the nod and they continued.

They hadn't gone far when they were confronted with the most heinous of sights. This time, it was a large dinosaur that Jake recognized as a stegosaurus. It was on its side, eyes closed, stomach ripped open, insides hanging out.

Jake could tell that this body must've been killed recently because the flies had yet to swarm it.

Hainey stood still as Jake approached to get a closer look.

"We're not far now," he called back to Hainey.

Hainey could barely get the words out, but when she did, it was enough to spur Jake into action.

"Jake," she screamed. "Run!"

3

Terrance walked over to Max and sat down next to him on the bench.

"How's your arm?"

Max didn't answer. Instead, he slid to his right, away from Terrance.

This sort of thing used to bother Terrance, but he'd seen it so many times now that he was getting used to it.

"How do you think Hainey and Jake are doing?" Terrance asked. He held his arm up to his face like he was checking the time on his watch, though he wasn't wearing one. "According to my calculations they've been gone... a long time."

Max again didn't answer, nor did he laugh at Terrance's attempt at humor. Had he had more room on the bench to slide over he would have. And had he had the energy and the ability to stand up and walk outside, he would have done that too.

"Not much of a talker are you?"

Max turned his head now, in a defiant little protest of Terrance, and looked at the opposite wall.

"Well look, buddy boy, you think you've got it bad? You don't have it half as bad as me. Do you know how long I've been out here waiting, hoping, wishing, praying for someone to come help me out of this?"

When Max didn't answer, Terrance took it upon himself to continue.

"I've been out here ten times as long as you've been alive? That's right, when your grandparents were your parents' age, I was here trying to figure out how in the heck I was going to get back to my parents. And, you know what the worst part of this whole thing has been? You might think it was crying myself to sleep at night, wondering why my parents weren't here by my side; you might think it was having to climb trees to escape all of the wild animals; you might think it was starving to death right here in the very spot this hut has been erected. And as bad as those things were, nothing shook me worse than what happened on the night of my death.

"Dying's a weird thing you know. I suppose it's probably different for everyone, depending on a number of different things: how you've lived your life, the choices you've made, who you're leaving behind, and how old you are, etcetera. But you know, when I died, I got to see my parents. It was just for a moment, just long enough to let me know that they had drown in the ocean while looking for me. Can you imagine how that makes a person feel? The kind of guilt it puts inside of one's heart? I've been stuck here knowing that the only way I'm ever going to see my parents again is if this place decides to release my soul to the great wherever. So what do you think about that? Not that you can do anything about it now. I just had to tell somebody, you know what I mean?"

Terrance stood up and walked out of the hut, leaving Max to wonder where in the world Hainey and Jake were, and what was taking them so long.

4

Jake knew he should have seen it coming. All the bodies stacked up and in various levels of decomposition should've been enough to alert him that there was a predator in their midst.

The tyrannosaurus was much larger than Jake had thought; easily as tall as his house. And fast. In no time flat, the mammoth collection of bones, muscle and teeth was on him.

Even with the stegosaurus between them, the rex had managed to get around it and onto Jake's scent faster than Jake would've thought possible.

Branches and twigs were taking swipes at his face as he continued to run no where in particular, forgetting momentarily about Hainey, realizing that he was only good to her if he, himself, was alive.

In the distance he saw a cave of sorts. It was really just a few massive rocks that had butted up against each other, creating a small opening that was large enough for a human, but not for a rex.

Jake ran in between them quickly and didn't turn around until he was sure that he was well out of striking distance. Each of the rocks went on for at least ten feet. So long as the rex wasn't able to tip them over, Jake was confident that he was safe for the moment.

As he looked out in the direction he'd just come, it was impossible to see anything with the tyrannosaur's snout covering the opening to the cave.

The rocks shook back and forth, giving Jake an uneasy feeling. He put his hands out against the walls, not really sure it would do any good. The rex continued to butt its head into the opening, forcing the rocks to shake more violently each time.

Jake closed his eyes and, fearing this might be the end, he began to pray. It was nothing major, really. No form prayer or anything he'd learned in church. Just a very simple, 'God, if I get out of here alive, I will do everything you want me to do from now on.'

And then he remembered Hainey, who was still out there.

Jake knew that he would be safe from the rex for hours if the rocks held up. But Jake didn't feel like he had hours. He thought he might have minutes at most.

Turning toward the back of the cave, he saw another opening. This one had light shining through it and he knew he had to head toward it and get Hainey.

Coming out of the cave from the opposite side felt oddly liberating. Jake was sure to keep himself out of the rex's view as he inched his way away from the rocks and found he was able to run behind a couple of trees.

The rex hadn't seen him and was still furiously slamming its head against the rock structure that Jake could not explain.

He looked around the edge of the tree and saw Hainey still standing in front of the stegosaurus, her hands up to her mouth like she was chewing her nails feverishly.

He thought better about moving his arms in an effort to garner her attention. Drawing the attention of the rex at this stage would be absolutely dastardly.

And then, as if they were living in a nightmare, another rex, this one much larger than the first, came around the corner of the stegosaurus and positioned itself directly behind Hainey.

She had to have heard it, Jake thought. The *thud, thud, thud* of its footsteps were so heavy, making the ground shake beneath their feet that there was no way Hainey didn't know it was there.

"Hainey," Jake yelled, breaking his silence, not caring if the first rex heard him or not. "Behind you!"

Hainey glanced behind herself and started to scream, running toward Jake as fast as she could.

She didn't get far, however. The first rex turned and began chasing her in the opposite direction and a third rex came racing out of the bushes at her.

Jake had to do something, and fast.

The tooth.

If he could find the tooth, it would bring them back to the hut. All he had to do was find it before Hainey was devoured.

He took off running in the direction of the stegosaurus. All three tyrannosaurs had come from that direction. Surely the tooth was back there somewhere.

It was hard for Jake to keep focused on his mission, with the devastating footsteps that were chasing after Hainey. And then Hainey's cries for help ringing in his ears.

But he knew this was the way. It had to be.

It didn't take long, a matter of a minute or two, and he was safely behind the stegosaurus, in the middle of a small thicket. Sure enough, the tooth was there, glowing, and begging him to pick it up and transport them back.

He grabbed it hard, not wasting a second. It was much larger than the other teeth they'd retrieved, roughly half the size of Jake. And heavy.

Something else was different about this tooth.

When Jake touched it, he was still in exactly the same place. He rubbed his hand along the tooth, trying to make sure the tooth knew that he was there. And then he gave the tooth a squeeze.

Nothing.

And then he looked out at the three tyrannosaurs chasing his five year old partner and he realized there was no way he could save them alone. He needed Hainey to grab on to the tooth as well.

5

How in the world could he possibly get Hainey out of the situation she was in and over to the tooth in one piece?

Think, Jake, think.

Bones.

That was it.

He took off down the path a little ways, running as fast as he could. He found the bones that they'd tripped over and picked up a hefty stack of them. They were heavy, but he forced himself to keep running back.

Hainey was still screaming and running, a good sign.

Jake went back into the clearing where the dinosaurs were having difficulty sharing. He was convinced that Hainey was still alive because the massive creatures were incapable of coordinating their attack. Unlike the raptor, there was no communication amongst the rexes. They chased the girl haphazardly and ran into each other.

One of them fell down and was rendered a non-threat for several minutes while it struggled to get up.

The other two continued to chase. Hainey had turned herself around and was running toward Jake.

"Keep it up Hainey!" he shouted. "Behind the stego, the tooth's back there!"

Jake dropped the bones at his feet and kept one in his right hand. As Hainey got closer he hurled the bone up at one of the tyrrannosaurs' noses. It stunned the creature momentarily. Not

long, but long enough for it to stop briefly to try
to figure out what had just happened.

Jake did the same thing to the other one,
hitting it right on its massive snout.

Hainey had taken off behind the stegosaurus
and Jake ran fast to join her.

"We don't have long," Jake said. "They'll be
back on us in no time."

"Okay, what do we do?" Hainey said, sucking
air.

"You get one side, I'll take the other. I tried to
get this one on my own, but I couldn't. I think it
might be too big for one person to handle."

Hainey nodded and gripped her end of the
tooth.

Jake grabbed his end.

And they were gone.

6

"Where are they?" Terrance mumbled as he paced back and forth.

He'd been walking in a small oval for a while now and Max was starting to feel really annoyed by the whole thing. He didn't want to be out in the jungle anymore, in the danger. But that was looking like a good alternative to watching Terrance kick up dirt and listening to him complain, not to mention that being around Terrance was really freaking him out.

"They should have been able to get it done by now —"

No sooner had Terrance spoken those words, than a vicious wind infiltrated the hut, blowing papers and dust all over. Max and Terrance had to shield their eyes.

"What is that?" Max yelled over the noise. It was like a freight train driving right by them.

Terrance smiled. "That's them. They're back!"

A moment later, Jake emerged through the door and announced, "We have done it!"

Terrance ran out to see what Hainey and Jake had brought back. Max continued to sit on the bench.

"Do you want to go out have a look?" Jake asked Max.

"No thank you."

Jake understood. If he'd had to sit around here with Terrance all that time, he'd probably need a break too.

"This is great!" Terrance was saying as Jake came back out to join Hainey. "What a massive tooth! There's no way I could've gotten this by myself."

Jake stood there, watching Terrance examine every inch of the tooth. He didn't want to seem rude, but he was definitely ready to get going and he was wondering when that time was going to come.

"Say," he said, "Terrance?"

Terrance stopped examining the tooth long enough to look up.

"When do you think we're going to be able to get out of here?"

7

Terrance's face changed.

Jake thought everything had been going so well these past few days, but now it seemed that the Terrance from earlier in the journey was going to come out one last time.

"No one leaves this place until I leave this place. I've seen so many kids like you come in here and do a few little tasks and then 'poof.'" Terrance made a little exploding motion with his fingers. "Out of sight, out of mind. Everyone always leaves before me and I'm sick of it." Terrance pointed a finger at Jake and Hainey. "The only way you're going to get what you want is if I get what I want!"

Jake and Hainey didn't say a word. Hainey moved closer to Jake and grabbed hold of him around his waist, hiding behind him.

Terrance walked away from the tooth and started pointing to the sky.

"Haven't I done everything? Haven't I done everything for you? I have! I have done everything you've asked me to do; every challenge you've put in front of me, I've met. Fifty years. Isn't that long enough? Haven't I suffered enough for you? Fifty years you've kept me in this wretched jungle, dangling your little carrot in front of my face, making me put kids through test after test after test after test. And now, I've done it. I've gotten the last tooth, I've convinced them that everything will be fine for them if they just help me and you're going to what...?"

Terrance dropped to his knees, his face touching the ground in front of him, hands clenching fistfuls of grass. He was muttering something under his breath, but neither Jake, nor Hainey could make out what it was.

There was a flash of brilliant light, like lightning, but all encompassing.

And then Terrance was gone.

8

Jake and Hainey stood in shocked silence for a minute. Then they ran into the hut to check on Max. But when they stepped inside, Max was gone, as was the bench and any other evidence that there had ever been a person living in there.

Hainey grabbed Jake's hand and the two walked out to examine the spot Terrance had just disappeared from.

There was nothing there. Not so much as a spot that would prove that he had ever lived in this jungle at all, or any bent blades of grass that would indicate that Terrance as sitting here a moment ago.

Jake turned back toward the hut, trying to put all the pieces together. But when he did, the hut was gone, and so were the chicken coups, and the fire pit...and the teeth. Everything was gone.

"You don't suppose..." he let his voice trail off at the thought that he and Hainey could possibly be the new Terrance of the jungle. It was too much to handle. There was an ache in his stomach now. He had nothing to throw up, but he hunched over and wretched at the thought anyway.

Hainey was sobbing and she dropped to her knees.

When Jake had finished heaving, he joined her on the ground and put his arm around her.

"It's going to be okay," he said to her one last time.

And then they were both gone.

9

Jake Lennon sits next to his mother at gate D. She's moving her legs up and down uncontrollably. The excitement she feels is too much for her to handle. She has a crossword puzzle book that she's purchased at the airport bookstore in one hand, the cover folded behind the book, giving her access to the first puzzle. She's written one word in ten minutes and is now anxiously tapping her pen on the puzzle.

"Oh, I can't do this now," she says, finally putting the book in her carry-on bag. "I'm just too excited Jake!"

She reaches out and grabs him by the arm and rocks him back and forth, seemingly trying to transfer some of her excitement to him.

It doesn't work.

He has no interest in going on this trip, whatsoever. He's wanted to stay home and play video games with his friends. And she knows it. He's complained endlessly, but her answer has always been, "Oh, Jake, you're going to love it. It's going to be a real wilderness experience!" She can't understand why that doesn't excite him. And the harder he rails against the trip, the more his mother has insisted that he go.

At one point, he thought he was going to get to stay with his uncle, but that had been short lived. It had been his father who put the kibosh on that one. He'd told his mother something about teaching their son the meaning of doing things as a family and opening yourself up to new experiences and blah, blah, blah.

Jake's attention is diverted from his loathing by a giggle. It's high pitched and way too happy for him to relate to. The source of the laughter is a young girl, who's holding tight to a pink Dora backpack as her mother laughs and pretends to take away her stuffed animal.

At least someone's having a good time.

He allows his eyes to move over to another kid. This boy doesn't appear to be having a good time. He doesn't appear to be having as miserable a time as Jake either. But Jake can't help but notice his parents. *Just leave the poor kid alone*, he thinks. His parents are wiping his nose and tying his shoes and checking his bag and rechecking his bag and asking him if he's okay. They ask him if he's hungry, if he's thirst, if he's had too much to eat, if he's had too much to drink, if he needs to use the bathroom, if he needs to pee, if he needs to poop. The list goes on and on and once Jake gets over the fact that his parents are a whole heap too overbearing, he actually finds it kind of funny and allows himself to smirk.

"Is that a smile I see?" his mother asks.

"No," Jake says and then he goes back to frowning, not wanting to give his mother the satisfaction.

"Honey, you wouldn't believe what I just found in the airport bookstore. It's the new James Patterson! I didn't think it was supposed to be out until next week, but somehow they have copies here right now!" He holds up the book which upsets his mother on two fronts.

The first is that he paid thirty dollars for three hundred pages of sub par entertainment.

Jake rolls his eyes at this thought, as he looks at his mother's crossword puzzle, which has been priced at ten dollars, and which she has completed one problem on one puzzle before deciding to put it away.

The other issue his mother is having with the book is the title and the cover. *Wreckage.* That's the title. Jake smirks again as he takes a good hard look at the cover and sees a plane wreck in the middle of a tree somewhere in the middle of a jungle.

10

"That's the book you're going to bring onto the plane?" Jakes mother asks.

"Uh-huh," his father nods, oblivious to her point.

"A book about a plane crash?"

"Yeah, why? What's wrong with that?"

"Nothing, I guess," his mother says, turning her head and crossing her legs. Her top leg is bobbing up and down. Jake makes a mental note that it's not as fast as he's seen it move before, but it's definitely at the top end of her leg bobbing tempo. He decides that he's going to stop talking about his issues with the trip until after they've landed safely.

His father gives him a nudge on the arm and gives a little chortle as Jake looks at him. For the moment, anyway, Jake finds this funny.

When his father is done having his chuckle, he takes the dust jacket off the book, places it on the seat next to him and starts leafing through the first few pages.

"This is going to be a real page turner," he notes to himself, happy with his selection.

Jake allows his eyes to wander and is struck suddenly when he looks to the boarding desk. There is a man with an airline issued suit and a name tag. He's looking at a computer screen, smiling.

Something about this man feels strange to Jake, familiar somehow.

The man picks up the intercom and announces, "We are now boarding Gate D. Gate D will be boarding at this time."

"That's us," Jakes mother smiles and taps his leg.

His father fumbles with the dust jacket for a moment before wrapping it properly onto the book and standing up.

They are toward the end of the line as a result.

As they move closer, Jake notices that the man is changing before his very eyes. He seems to be shrinking with every ticket he inspects.

"Have a great trip!" he says to one woman.

"You're going to love it there," he comments to the man after her.

A third person hands him a ticket and by now the change is noticeable. "Enjoy yourself," he tells the man.

Jake tugs on his mother's arm. "Mom, do you see that?"

His mother looks where Jake is pointing.

"See what?"

"The man taking the tickets, is there something...weird?"

"Jake," his mother scolds him. "Don't be rude. He seems like a very nice man."

Jake turns to ask his father, but his father is fully engrossed in his book, and seems to be paying attention to little else.

By the time Jake turns back, the man taking the tickets has changed into a boy of about fifteen years old. No one in the line seems to notice anything.

It's his mother's turn to hand the boy her ticket. "You are absolutely going to love it there," the boy smiles at his mother as he gives her back the ticket.

It's now Jake's turn. And the boy has completed his transformation. He looks familiar to Jake, but Jake is unable to place him.

He guesses the boy is about twelve years old. Jake looks down at his outfit and notices that he is no longer wearing the airline issued suit. Rather, he is wearing a hoodie and jeans.

Jake hands him the ticket and looks to the few people in line left behind them. Have they noticed? None of them seem to be acting like anything out of the ordinary is happening.

"Is it your first time going to the jungle?" the boy asks.

Jake nods.

"I think you're going to absolutely love it. So many different animals to encounter."

Jake studies the boy one last time, noticing his dark eyes. He knows he's seen him before, seen that smile, seen those eyes.

The boy hands Jake his ticket. "Enjoy the flight," he says, a dark smile forming on his lips. He gives Jake a wink and says, "I'll be seeing you real soon."

GET YOUR FREE BOOK!

For your free copy of the #1 Best Seller Farty Marty,
go to www.justinjohnsonauthor.com

Books I've Written

Coby Collins
Coby Collins and the Hex Bolt of Doom
Coby Collins and the Diary of Tingledowner
Coby Collins and the Tunnels of Marley
Coby Collins and the Battle at Bale

Scab and Beads: Locket's Away
Scab and Beads: Milk Mayhem
Scab and Beads: Homework Heist

Grade School Super Hero
Grade School Super Hero: Here We Go Again
Grade School Super Hero: Just Another Day
Grade School Super Hero: The Complete Trilogy

Zack and Zebo: The Complete Series

The Jungle: The Complete Series

The Card

Short Stories
Farty Marty and Other Stories (Collection)
Do Not Feed the Zombies and Other Stories (Collection)
The Disgusting and Heartwarming Collection
Farty Marty: A Heartwarming Tale of Farts and Friendship
Do Not Feed the Zombies
Skeeter Skunk and the Glandular Funk
Ricky Raccoon and the Huge Dumpster Dive
The Dance Recital
Flick!
The Kick
Sarah and the Search for the Pot of Gold
A Kid in King William's Court

ABOUT THE AUTHOR

I am a teacher in Fulton, NY. I write stories for the students I teach. I live in Hastings, NY with my family.

For information on new releases check out:
www.justinjohnsonauthor.com

43512398R00173

Made in the USA
San Bernardino, CA
19 December 2016